Praise for **TANEESHA NEVER DISPARAGING**

"A **FAST-PACED** portrait of a girl grounded in
her Buddhist practice and loving family, coping
with the daily struggles of growing up."
—Kathe Koja, author of *Buddha Boy*

"Taneesha's voice is **FRESH, FUNNY**, and **TRUE** as a
lotus blossom in a muddy pond. Readers will become
familiar with Nichiren Buddhism—and the word
disparaging—as Taneesha navigates her way through fifth
grade as a Buddhist, daughter, and good friend to all."
—Kelly Easton, author of *Hiroshima Dreams*

"**A JOY TO READ.** This book addresses the
issues many kids face today with a fresh and
positive perspective. Don't miss this beautifully
and skillfully written novel."
—David Richardson, columnist for *Reading Today*

"I will definitely use this as a '**BOOK OF THE MONTH**'
IN MY CLASSROOM. I can hardly
wait for the next installment!"
—Magnolia Walker, reading teacher
(4th and 5th Grades), Crawford County
Elementary School in Roberta, Georgia

"**INSPIRATION**

—Midwest Book Revi

Taneesha Never Disparaging

TANEESHA NEVER DISPARAGING

by M. LaVora Perry

Wisdom Publications • Boston

Wisdom Publications
199 Elm Street
Somerville MA 02144 USA
www.wisdompubs.org

Library of Congress Cataloging-in-Publication Data
Perry, M. LaVora.
 Taneesha Never Disparaging / by M. LaVora Perry.
    p. cm.
 Summary: Teased and tormented because of her choice of friends, her Buddhist
religion, and her lackluster campaign for class president, Taneesha's fifth-grade
school year proves to be disappointing until she learns to make peace with herself
and those around her.
 ISBN 0-86171-550-0 (pbk. : alk. paper)
 [1. Buddhism—Fiction. 2. Bullies—Fiction. 3. Schools—Fiction. 4. African
Americans—Fiction.] I. Title.
 PZ7.P4353Tan 2008
 [Fic]—dc22

                                                  2008016710

12 11 10 09 08
5 4 3 2 1

Cover illustration by Floyd Cooper.
Cover design by Tony Lulek, Josh Bartok, and Rod Meade Sperry. Interior design by
Tony Lulek and Josh Bartok. Set in Johanna MT 13/16.

Wisdom Publications' books are printed on acid-free paper and meet the
guidelines for permanence and durability of the Production Guidelines for
Book Longevity of the Council on Library Resources.

Printed in Canada

To my husband, Cedric Richardson, and my parents, Mattie and Rudolph Perry, for always supporting and believing in my dreams; to my children, Nia, Jarod, and Jahci for calling Taneesha out to play; and to every reader who has stood by this girl from day one—thank you.

CONTENTS

Guaranteed Public Humiliation   1

The "I'm-Not-Running-
    for-Any-Dang-Thing" Plan   11

Bonked on the Head   23

Bloody & Beaten on Bernard   31

Showtime at the Bey-Ross'   42

E.T. Meets Six X-Ray Eyes   52

No Parents Home   64

They Had Been to Hell   76

Song of an Old Friend   87

Human-Eating Bigfoot   94

Flouncing Out   106

DOWNRIGHT DANGEROUS FLORIDA 115

GAGGING UP GUAVA-MANGO JUICE 131

THE MEAN LAUGH 139

DRESSED LIKE A CANDIDATE 150

SNAKE SNACK 160

INVISIBLE, COZY BLANKET 170

STANDING O 180

ACKNOWLEDGMENTS 195

ABOUT THE AUTHOR 199

X

CHAPTER 1

GUARANTEED PUBLIC HUMILIATION

There I was, scribbling Taneesha Bey-Ross, Monday, January 7, 2008, across the top of a fresh page in my writing notebook, without a clue that chaos was just minutes away. I looked through a classroom window at the freezing outside—cloudy, like it was all the time lately, with snow on the ground and everything. But you'd never have known it in Room 509 of North Cleveland's Jane Hunter Elementary School. Toasty. Just the way I like it. So toasty that even though I'd forgotten to wear a sweater, I stayed warm in my "dress-code" get-up—white blouse, navy blue pants, black shoes.

1

I looked around at the astronomy sculptures, geometry mobiles, and A and B+ papers that decorated the walls, shelves, and ceiling. With a leg stretched out, I silently bounced a rubber heel on the blue-grey carpet, the kind for inside and outside, and breathed in its new-car smell. Glad to be back in 509.

It was the first day of school after Winter Break and I'd actually wanted to get back to Hunter. The break had been getting boring. Nothing to do.

So there I sat, scribbling with one hand and tangling the fingers of the other in the nappy tip of one of my twisty African locks.

"And so, fifth graders—" Trim Mr. Alvarez, who had the exact same tan as the oat flakes I'd had for breakfast over three hours ago, pointed to the list of words he'd written on the chalkboard:

Gratitude, Compassion, Perseverance, Courage, Wisdom, Cheerfulness.

"These are just some character traits that good leaders possess. Keep them in mind when you

2

consider who to nominate for class officers in our coming election."

I couldn't help thinking how Mr. Alvarez was always so sharp. Today his short, coal-black hair looked especially shiny. Like he'd Vaselined it up or something. Neatly combed, of course. He had on this crisp, beige shirt, a dark blue necktie and matching suit pants. The crease in his pants could have sliced a hunk of cold cheddar cheese.

For some reason, the more I stared at Mr. Alvarez's crisp, beige shirt, the more I thought of whole grain wafers.

My stomach gave a long growl. I quickly swept my eyes around the room and saw Rayshaun Parker, a hefty kid, look at me and then look away, bored. Good. That would have been all I needed—Rayshaun catching me growling. It seemed like he hadn't heard my stomach. Nobody else seemed to either. Thank goodness.

Now that Rayshaun was in my head, he parked his irritating self there. Great. Mainly, that boy and I only talked to each other when we had to. You would have never known we used to be best friends back in the day, in kindergarten.

See, one time, back then, Rayshaun and I were playing House together in the little kitchen area in our classroom. He was the daddy and I was the mommy. Rayshaun was clobbering a baby doll's back over his shoulder, "burping" it. It was one of those dolls whose hair is really just molded plastic.

He picked that particular doll for our "daughter" because he said her skin looked like the chocolate outside of an ice-cream sandwich just like mine. He said that since she was just a baby it didn't matter that she didn't have cornrow braids or lips like me (she basically had no lips; I have plenty). Our "son" was always this little white doll that looked more like Rayshaun—just without his nappy hair.

The whole "family" thing was all Rayshaun's idea, not mine, since he wanted to marry me and I wasn't sure I felt the same way about him. But I liked to play House though.

So there he was, pounding our poor daughter's back, while I stood at the ironing board ironing a red-and-white cotton bandana—the kind farmers and gang members wear. The iron wasn't hot or anything, of course. It didn't even have a plug.

All of a sudden, Rayshaun stopped whopping that doll, looked straight at me, and said, "Taneesha Bey-Ross, my mother says you going to hell because you ain't Christian."

Rayshaun's hair wasn't black like most kids'. It was this dusty brown like somebody had dumped a bucket of sand over it and he'd shook it off—only some stayed.

When he told me I was going to hell, I'd felt like he'd dumped dirt all over me. But I couldn't shake it off. I didn't let him know I felt that way, though.

After school that day, I stood in my kitchen and cried, "Mama, why'd you tell?!"

The week before, my mother had come to my class for Cultural Traditions Day. She brought food like other parents did—collard greens. She talked about how African American slaves ate them back in the day and how collards were healthy because they had a lot of fiber and more calcium than a cup of milk. All the kids kept saying her greens tasted good and that we looked just alike, except I was a pretzel stick and she had a shape.

But Alima Ross couldn't leave it at that. Oh, no, not my mother. True to form, she had to go all extreme and tell everybody about our family's unique little tradition.

"Mama, why'd you tell we're *Buddhist*?!" I'd screamed in the kitchen. "Rayshaun said his mother says I'm going to hell!"

Mama had had on a nurse's uniform—a scrub top and pants—that was pinkish red like grapes. She stooped down and made her dark brown face even with mine. I smelled apples in the grayish afro puff on her head. With a white ball of Kleenex in her hand, she started wiping away the tears and snot that ran down my face.

"Taneesha," she said, "I'm so sorry Rayshaun said that to you. But sweetie, hell and heaven aren't places. They're right in here." She patted my chest. "Buddhahood is too. Do you know what that is?"

I sniffed and shook my head. I thought Mama might have told me what Buddhahood was before but I couldn't remember.

"It's happiness that's as big as the whole universe. And when you chant Nam Myoho Renge Kyo, you make it come out."

She told me to chant for Rayshaun and his mother to be happy.

Mama and I chanted together at the altar in our living room and that made me feel okay.

Oh, the simple mind of a kindergartner. I'd actually thought that would be it. Chant and the world would go back to normal.

But what really happened was this: For a long time—on the school playground, in the lunchroom, standing in line, whenever and wherever he could—Rayshaun, who was chubby back then, not solid like he is now, kept following behind me, saying "You going to *hell*, Taneesha. You better get *saved*."

I never told our teacher. I was afraid if the other kids found out what Rayshaun said, they'd agree with him.

And I didn't say anything more to Mama about it either. Even when she asked. I just acted like it was all over.

Why'd I do that? For one thing, her chanting idea had obviously been a big fat *dud*. For another, I didn't want her coming up to Hunter to talk to Rayshaun because then my whole class would have *definitely* found out about the whole situation.

So I'd just whisper back at that boy, "No I'm

not going to hell, Rayshaun Parker. Hell's not a place, it's inside."

After a while, he stopped bugging me. But we never went back to being friends like before. Far from it. Whenever Rayshaun got the chance, he'd laugh at something dumb I did.

Guaranteed public humiliation: one more reason why what was coming next in Room 509 was totally out of the question.

I glanced at the clock. I wondered how long we had 'til lunch. I imagined chowing down on a cool slice of cheese laid out on a piece of Mr. Alvarez's crunchy shirt.

"Now, let's get started on the task at hand," he said, looking mighty cheesy. "Are there any nominations for class president?"

CARLI FLANAGAN, YOU STOP THAT RIGHT NOW!

A terrifying sight ripped me from my cheddary daydream—Carli's hand shooting up into the air. I wanted to scream at that girl flat out, instead of only in my suddenly splitting-headachy head.

I would have screamed, too, if it weren't for the fact that I'd have looked crazy.

I had a sick feeling about that puny, pale hand, all dotted with brown freckles. It was my best friend Carli's hand, a hand that was eleven years old—just like mine. That hand flapped wildly over Carli's wavy, red hair. With each flap, she wriggled in her seat so much that the metal brace on her left leg clunked against the metal of her desk's leg. But she didn't even notice the clunking. She was too busy flapping.

"*Psssst!*" I whispered, "Carli! *Carli!*" as loudly as I could without drawing Mr. Alvarez's attention. I hoped with everything I had that Carli wouldn't do what I thought she would if I didn't stop her in time.

Desperate, I started going: "Nam Myoho Renge Kyo! Nam Myoho Renge Kyo! Nam Myoho Renge Kyo!..." like a chanting machine.

I bet my parents would have loved knowing I was doing that—even if it was just silently.

Hmmph. As if I'd sit up in class chanting out loud.

But maybe I should have. Because my way didn't work.

Next thing I knew, I heard Carli saying, "I nominate Taneesha Bey-Ross for president!"

9

Pudgy, caramel-brown Kendra Adams seconded the nomination. And that was that.

Once the whole class saw me get nominated, I was too embarrassed to say I wouldn't run.

Don' t worry. You won' t win anyway. Losers never do.

For once, I actually hoped Evella was right. She's my evil twin—totally imaginary but a major butt-pain anyway. I nicknamed her Evella a while back. Anyway, I hoped she was right— not about me being a loser, of course, but about me not winning. I didn't want to be class president. It was hard enough just being me.

Trapped in my seat, all I could do was tangle my fingers in the tip of one of my locks. And cook up an escape plan.

CHAPTER 2

THE "I'M-NOT-RUNNING-FOR-ANY-DANG-THING" PLAN

After school, in the cloudy daylight, I walked up Bernard Avenue with Carli, who was just a little shorter and meatier than me. We had to walk because we weren't eligible to ride a school bus since our parents had signed us up to go to Hunter even though both of us lived closer to other schools. We were bundled in our puffy winter coats—mine was the silvery-purple one I'd gotten in November when, thanks to global warming, the weather had just started getting cooler. Carli's coat was pink. We both had on scarves, gloves, and boots. I wore ear-muffs and an extra pair of socks. I hate Jack Frost nipping at my nose so I don't take chances.

I couldn't wait to make it to Rosebush Road—a street lined on both sides with mini-mansions that this rich guy named John D. Rockefeller built in the 1900s. Walking, I remembered Mama saying our red-brick house—the tiniest one on Rosebush—was just the right size for our family.

Carli and I walked on packed, dirty, days-old snow that hid parts of milk cartons, broken glass bottles, and pieces of crumpled McDonald's french-fry holders. We passed houses—some rickety or boarded up, others in okay shape, some looking good. Covered in snow, even the worst ones looked better than usual. Before we'd get to my house, we'd walk ten blocks and cross Aristotle Avenue—U.S. Route 20, just a few miles south of Lake Erie.

It's uphill from Bernard to Rosebush. But you don't really feel it so much when you're walking, only when you're riding a bike and pedaling against gravity—a bike like the beautiful magenta one I'd gotten over the summer, when it was warm and sunny, and I was just plain old Taneesha, not anybody's candidate.

While I mentally hammered out the details of my I'm-not-running-for-any-dang-thing plan, I looked at all the traffic crossing Aristotle two blocks ahead of us. Aristotle, a main roadway, was in the middle of a major upgrade that included a wider street and new sidewalks, street signs, and bus shelters. I remembered my father saying Aristotle ran east and west from Massachusetts to Oregon.

"Taneesha," Carli said, interrupting my thought-flow, "for your campaign, I was thinking I could ask my aunt Bridgid to make some of her candy. It's always a big hit at the bazaars they have at her church. We could pass it out with 'Taneesha's the Sweetest!' buttons. What do you think?"

Why, I wondered, was Carli asking for my opinion now? It was a little late for that, wasn't it? Since she'd already up and nominated me.

"Candy sounds nice."

You are such a wimp.

Just what I needed—Evella's expert opinion.

"Watch it, shrimp!"

I looked up. Standing right in the middle of the sidewalk—not on one side or the other, which would have been the courteous, *human* thing to do—stood an ogre.

Her face was like a broad, brown crayon with eyes. A swarm of poisonous spikes, skinny extension braids, poked from underneath her knitted skullcap. It was blood red, just like her bulging jacket—a jacket that bulked up a body that seemed more than big enough already. Black backpack straps cut into the red of her jacket. Dark blue slacks clung to her thick legs. And, like bulletproof armor, long, wide army boots covered the two tanks that almost passed for feet.

"I'm talking to *you*. And you, *too*, white girl."

Do you think she needed to say it twice?

Like the Red Sea in that cartoon movie, *The Prince of Egypt*, Carli parted to one side and I swerved to the other.

We went back to walking up Bernard—slower than I wanted to, considering how the Beasty One had just barked at us. But I had to creep along so Carli could keep up since she had that metal brace on her left leg and limped a little.

Neither of us talked about what had just

14

happened. Probably, like me, Carli wanted to be out of that girl's hearing range.

"Some people," she whispered when we made it to the corner of Aristotle and Bernard.

"Yeah," I said, with absolutely no feeling. "Some people."

I wasn't really thinking about the girl anymore. I'd gone back to tinkering with my I'm-not-running plan. I hadn't been able to really focus on it in school because there were too many distractions—math, science, lunch, all that stuff. But now the plan was taking shape—and yanking my parents' strings was a big part of it.

Had I known better, instead of wasting all my brain cells on the nomination, which was nothing compared to what was coming, I would have been thinking up ways to get the heck out of Dodge before that big brown ogre—Shrek untamed—landed on me.

"She's probably from Legacy," Carli said.

"Hunh?"

"That girl. She's probably from Legacy Middle School. You know how teenagers always think they're all that."

"Oh. Yeah. Right."

15

"Why so quiet?"

Carli and I had just crossed over to the south side of Aristotle and I couldn't bring myself to tell her what I was really thinking: "Girl, are you *nuts*?! My life is careening down Disaster Street because you nominated me!"

"Oh. No reason. Just thinking." I wasn't totally lying. I didn't have time for chit-chat. I needed to put the final touches on my plan to reverse the damage Carli had done. "I'm just ready to get home, that's all."

"Nam Myoho Renge Kyo. Nam Myoho Renge Kyo. Nam Myoho Renge Kyo."

At the start of dinner, Mama, Daddy, and I finished doing Sansho together, chanting three times. We sat at our oak kitchen table with four yellow walls around us.

I had changed into a purple sweatsuit and the smell of stewed tomatoes, onions, garlic, and veggies had me ready to eat. Wiggling my toes, I noticed that the pot of pinto bean soup simmering on the stove warmed every part of our small kitchen including the wooden floor underneath my lavender bunny slippers.

"Taneesha, chant clearly," Mama said. Dark brown like Daddy and I, and curvier than either of us, she had a short, salt-n-pepper afro and wore a beige sweater. Her favorite pastime? Nagging me. "You were mumbling, sweetie," she said. "When you chant, *enunciate*. Each word has a meaning."

Whatever.

I didn't even say anything to that. Mama mentioning chanting reminded me that I was more than a little irked about the fact that Nam Myoho Renge Kyo failed me big time in school that day. I mean, I'd poured my guts into chanting not to be nominated and where'd that gotten me?

Anyway, even without chanting, I'd thunk up an excellent plan on the way home. I held back before I rolled it out, though.

I started slurping up soup, waiting for the perfect moment. If I worked it just right, I could get my parents to give me what I needed.

I looked from Mama to Daddy and took another slurp. Pinto beans and lots of carrots, zucchini, yellow squash, and chunks of tomatoes and onions. The weather outside made soup perfect for dinner. We had salad too, with romaine lettuce. I'd sliced the cucumbers and tomatoes and radishes for it.

17

"Marsha laid off two nurses today," Mama said. "Beverly and Drew."

"Well, you saw it coming, didn't you?" Daddy, the lanky man that everybody says I get my skinniness from, had a micro 'fro, not nearly as grey as Mama's, and was still in a white business shirt. He'd lost his tie, though. "You said last week somebody was up next," he said.

"Yeah. But I guess I hoped I was wrong. Two people, though. I didn't see *that* coming."

They kept talking like I wasn't there. That was okay; I needed time to practice my lines in my head.

"But if you're down two nurses, that's going to put a lot of pressure on you."

"Who're you telling?"

Daddy looked at Mama. "Things will pick up, honey." He reached across the table and put his hand on top of hers. "Thanks for hanging with me, Alima. Business has just been slow but it won't stay this way. I promise. Then you won't have to work all these hours."

Mama smiled at him. Her eyes looked into his and her face got deep red. "More chanting, baby," she said.

"Always."

That was good. They were getting all lovey-dovey. In a good mood—the perfect mood to say "Yes" to anything the one and only daughter they'd prayed for years and years to have asked them to do.

"Oh, Taneesha—" Mama said, without taking her eyes off Daddy, "before I forget, we're going to church this Sunday."

"Okay," I said, even though I knew she was so all into Daddy's eyes that she probably didn't hear me.

I slurped more soup and thought about Granddaddy's church, the church Mama and I went to, where people called Granddaddy "Elder" Ross instead of "Mr." Daddy hardly ever came with us on those Sundays because he went to Buddhist men's meetings instead.

At church, my head always wound up knocking against Mama's arm because I'd nod off to sleep. No matter how hard I tried, I couldn't stay awake the whole time.

I jabbed my fork into my salad, speared lettuce, tomato, and cucumber on it, and shoved it all into my mouth. I love ranch dressing.

Chewing, I thought about how Mama took me

to Granddaddy's church so I could "learn my roots" and I remembered how the whole thing got started.

I was maybe six or seven at the time. Wearing a blue jean jumpsuit, I'd had been laying stomach-down on the living room carpet at Big Mama and Granddaddy's house watching *That's So Raven* on cable. (We don't have cable at home so it's a perk of going to my grandparents'.) Anyway, Granddaddy and my mother were sitting on the other side of the living room from me. Big Mama was in the kitchen, cooking.

Deep brown and slim with yellowish-grey, fuzzy hair, Granddaddy sat in his easy chair wearing his usual: silver-wire-rimmed glasses, light brown slacks, a whitish shirt, brown suspenders, and black slippers. His same humungous Bible with gold letters stamped on its black leather cover lay open on his lap.

Mama sat across from him, barefoot, on the plastic-wrapped, white couch. She had on an orange and yellow tie-dyed African dress with no sleeves.

"Alima," Granddaddy had said, real even, "I don't care what you do or don't believe. Taneesha needs to know how we do."

When I heard my name, I kept still, tuned up my ears, glued my eyes to the TV—and pretended I wasn't eavesdropping.

"I'm not going to be around forever. It's just like the sun. It's high in the sky at noon, but come around four o'clock, it starts to set. There isn't anything we can do about that."

At that, I couldn't help it, I turned and looked at my mother. She seemed ready to speak. But then, it was like she changed her mind.

"That child needs to learn her roots," Granddaddy said.

Mama stayed quiet, like she was thinking hard.

I went back to staring at the TV but I couldn't even really see it. I couldn't hear it either. I wished I hadn't heard what Granddaddy had just said about the sun setting and everything. I wished he hadn't said it, but I knew he had.

Ever since that day, Mama and I've been going to church. But only once a month, not every Sunday the way some people do.

I speared another forkful of salad and thought about one time when I was moaning about going to church and Mama said, "Taneesha, it's good for you to learn what other people believe. It takes all kinds of people to make world peace. Not everybody's going to be Buddhist."

I laughed a little, real dry, just thinking about that one.

Mama and Daddy looked at me for a second, then went back to their ogling.

Not everybody's going to be Buddhist? Who had Mama been kidding? Mostly *nobody's* Buddhist. How could I not know that little fact when everybody else's religion is advertised all over the place—even on money?

Plus, what had Buddhism done for me lately? Today, for example? If the catastrophe Carli had set in motion was going to be undone, it wasn't *Buddhism* that was going to undo it. It was me, Taneesha Bey-Ross.

Speaking of which, it was about time to work my plan. My parents had stopped talking. No telling how long that would last. I put down my fork, cleared my throat, and dived in.

CHAPTER 3

BONKED ON THE HEAD

"Carli nominated me for class president."

"Good for you, Taneesha! I think you'll make a fine president," said Mama, snapping out of her lock-eyed trance with Daddy all like Cinderella's Fairy Godmother had just said, "Bibbidi-bobbidi-boo!" She had this big old grin on her face.

Was she out of her mind?

"But—"

"I think you'll make a good president, too, sweetie."

"But—"

"In fact, I think you'll make a *great* president,"

23

Daddy continued. "Think of being class president as preparation for when you have the big job: Taneesha Bey-Ross, President of the United States."

"Get real, Daddy." Why had I even bothered to tell them about this? I knew why: I needed their help.

"No, I'm serious," he said, dabbing the corner of his mouth with his napkin. "You're a natural leader, Taneesha."

Who in the world was he talking about?

"There's only one problem: I *don't want to do* it. I wish Carli had asked me before she nominated me."

"Well," said Daddy, "did you tell her that?"

"No." How could I? That would've hurt her feelings. She seemed so happy about gearing up for my campaign.

"She can't read your mind, you know," Mama said, as if she was reading my mind. "Are you going to tell her how you feel?"

"I don't want her to feel bad. I think she was trying to be nice."

"So what are you going to do?" asked Daddy. He slurped a spoonful of soup.

24

I felt a little sweaty. This was it. Time for me to spring my plan on them. Ready... Set... Go! "I was wondering if you could kind of, sort of— *write me a note.*"

They looked blank. Like they hadn't understood me.

"A note saying I can't be president."

Still nothing.

"And what would our reason be," Daddy said, *finally,* "in this note, for saying you can't be president?" On "president" he did this one-raised-eyebrow thingy he does a lot.

Did I know my parents, or what?

I had my comeback all ready:

"You could just say I have too much homework to do it. It's true, you know. I have lots of work. I wouldn't want my grades to slip because I'm trying to do too much. Being president is a big responsibility."

I looked hard at those two's faces, trying to read their expressions. And it seemed to me as if they were both fixing to laugh. At me.

Mama smiled.

Is she really going to help me out? Do I actually have a note on the way?

25

Then a chunk of my blue sky fell down and bonked me right on the head. *Hard.*

"Taneesha, I think you need to chant," she said.

Here we go! I hated having my problems, and I had plenty, boiled down to one word: "chant." If chanting worked so much, how come it had bombed in school that day?

"Mama, I don't need to chant. I need *help*. Didn't you *hear* me? I just want a little note. I told you how hard school is and everything. But all you two can do is laugh at me and tell me to chant!"

I couldn't stand how my parents threw chanting into everything. Sometimes it drove me nuts. It was like they couldn't hear me or something. Like they were talking robots that only went "Chant, chant, chant" no matter what I was saying.

"We weren't laughing at—"

"Oh come on, Daddy! Yes you were. You two always act like I'm a joke or something. Just once I wish you'd *listen* to me."

They looked at me like I was speaking gibberish.

"Okay," Daddy said after a moment. "We're listening."

26

I breathed in deep. "Like I said, I just want a note explaining everything. It doesn't have to be long. I just want you to tell Mr. Alvarez that this isn't a good time for me to try to run for anything."

I looked from Mama to Daddy, holding my breath, hoping to hear the one word that would make my life a little less crazy: "Okay."

But, looking at their faces, I started feeling like the band-leader on a sinking ship—frantically waving my baton while I was going down fast.

"You don't even have to write it," I blurted. "I'll write it and sign it!" I hadn't meant to squeak. It just came out that way.

"Honey," Mama said as if she was talking to a baby or something, "You're a big girl. Eleven years old. You can speak for yourself. Just tell Mr. Alvarez how you feel."

"But—"

"You just need confidence, Taneesha," Daddy said, all tender. "The way to get it is to keep chanting and doing your best."

They just didn't get it. I was drowning. Drowning, dagnamit.

"But—"

And all Daddy could say was: "Remember,

27

Nichiren said, 'A coward cannot have any of her prayers answered.'"

Whatever that meant.

"But—"

"When you forget who you are, Taneesha, you've got to chant harder," said Mama. "I think that's the problem. Your evil twin's just working on you."

Now she had to go talking about that.

"It's like I always say, everybody's got an evil twin yanking their chain. Your evil twin's job's to make you feel small—like you're not big as the universe. And she never takes a vacation. Your job's to remember you're all that and then some."

I dropped my shoulders. Didn't she see? The problem was, I didn't feel like "all that." Right then, I felt like one big nothing and her and Daddy acting like whatever I said didn't matter just made me feel nothinger.

But I knew I'd be wasting my time if I told them any of that. I knew they wouldn't have heard a word I said. They'd only go, "Chant. Chant. Chant."

"Let's chant after dinner, okay?" Mama said.

28

It would have been funny—only it wasn't.

Tears came.

"That's okay, Mama. I got a lot of homework." I pushed my chair away from the table. "I'm done eating." I stood and picked up my dishes.

Seconds later, I stood at the sink and rinsed silverware, plates, and bowls in the sink.

Watching white salad dressing and tomato-red broth swirl down the drain, I felt Mama and Daddy staring at me.

I stacked everything into the dishwasher.

I didn't need to see their faces to know they were sticking to their decision—even though I was dying.

I dragged my feet into the hallway.

How could they have possibly thought that tacking Nam Myoho Renge Kyo, or some dusty old quote from Nichiren—the ancient Japanese guy that made chanting famous—over my jumbled-up feelings would do any good? That's what I wanted to know. They'd have had better luck slapping a Band-Aid over the crack in the Grand Canyon.

"Taneesha," Mama said. "We love you."

"Yeah, right," I muttered.

"What did you say?" Daddy asked in a warning voice.

"I'm going to do my homework."

I kept dragging.

I heard Mama say something about not needing all this stress right now.

She didn't need stress? What about *me*? I was the one who was doomed—doomed to go back to Hunter Elementary tomorrow totally noteless.

CHAPTER 4

BLOODY & BEATEN
ON BERNARD

Fifth graders," said Mr. Alvarez, "in the North Cleveland City School District all students have the option of participating in Take Your Child To Work Day. Your parents must sign the note I gave you so I'll know if you'll be in school next Friday or not."

It was Monday morning and a full week had crawled by since Carli had nominated me for president. As usual, my life wasn't satisfied with just being bad, it had to get all horrendous on me. Plus, the report I'd gotten from Weather.com the night before had been wrong. It wasn't "partially cloudy" it was just plain old cloudy—*again*.

"Please raise your hand if you've already talked to your parents about visiting their places of employment next week."

A few hands went up, including Carli's. I'd always loved the navy blue jumper with silver heart-shaped buttons she was wearing—dress-code with class. But I didn't love it enough to forget that she was pretty much responsible for ruining any chance I might have had of having a happy fifth-grade experience.

While Carli looked all cute, raising her hand in her classy jumper, a girl in boring black jeans and a white blouse, sweater, and pair of sneakers, hid her very un-raised left hand in her lap.

I rolled my head upward blasé-style. My eyes followed the every-which-way patterns of the twenty geometry mobiles hanging from the ceiling—one from each student in the class. Each mobile was a mix of colorful shapes. Raspberry octagons. Orange hexagons. Aquamarine pentagons. Some shapes were made by gluing strips together. Others by cutting—the same as how you cut snowflakes and rows of dolls out of paper. No two designs were exactly alike. My mobile was mostly different shades of purple, my favorite color. I followed it with my eyes while it swayed a little in a breeze I didn't feel. I watched those mobiles like they were the only thing in the world, determined to do everything I could to sweep Take Your Child To Work Day right out of my mind. I hadn't said one word to my parents about that particular event. And I wasn't going to. Skipping school for a day sounded fun, but not if it meant I had to mingle with people I didn't know. Some people are natural minglers. I knew me; I wasn't one of them.

"Sorry, I can't get the candy from my aunt." Carli said, while we walked up Bernard Avenue after school on one more afternoon without sunshine—me in my puffy silvery-purple coat, Carli in her pink one.

"What candy?"

"For your campaign, girl. Come on, get with the program. Election day'll be here before you know it."

"Oh. That candy," I said, wishing I had a time machine so I could go back to the morning of the day Carli nominated me. At home, I would have run a thermometer under hot water and drank food coloring to make my throat look red. It worked once on picture day. That time, I stayed home with "the flu." If I had done it again, I could have avoided the whole election thing because absent kids couldn't be nominated.

"Carli?"

"Yeah?"

I opened my mouth. But then, I just couldn't do it. I couldn't tell her that I didn't want to run.

"What were you saying about candy?"

"My aunt's in the hospital. She had to get a hip operation. So she can't make it."

"Make what?"

"The *candy*."

"Oh. Right. Well, that's okay."

"Yeah. You're a strong candidate. You can win without candy. Everybody likes you and you really do have all those leadership traits Mr. Alvarez's been talking about."

"You're funny, Carli."

"I'm not trying to be funny. Sometimes I don't think you see how much, um... how much... um... *potential* you have."

"Like I said, you're funny, Carli."

"No. You're funny. But I like you anyway."

At that, I had to laugh. We both did.

"So anyway, I'm going to help my father in the pharmacy next Friday. What about you? You going to your father's job or your mother's?"

"Neither."

"How come?"

"Don't want to. It'll probably be boring."

"Your parents don't mind if you don't do it?"

"Don't know. Didn't ask them."

"But they have to sign the note—that's what Mr. Alvarez said."

"I know."

Now I'd said that all like I had everything under control. But the fact was I hadn't given one thought to getting that note signed. I had made up my mind: I was going to school next Friday and that was that.

"They'll sign it. I just didn't give it to them yet."

"Why you always got to be in my way?"

Dagnamit.

Shrek was back, rude as ever, blocking the sidewalk just like she'd done last week.

"Sorry," Carli and I said together.

35

"I *know* you sorry."

I looked into those two slits she used for eyes. It was probably in them right then—the hatred that would reach out and touch me in a real bad way pretty soon. But I was too simple-minded to see it for what it was. I thought that girl was just being cranky. Maybe on PMS like Mama always talked about. How could I have known then that she was just a plain-old devil?

Carli and I eased past her huge, red jacketness. I picked up my pace as much as I could considering Carli's limp.

"*Teenagers*," Carli whispered to me.

I looked over my shoulder.

"Yeah. Teenagers," I whispered back, even though Shrek was far enough down Bernard by then that there was no way she could have heard me.

Just then, I heard lots of people running behind me and before I could turn to see what was happening—

"You can run, but I'm still going to kick your ass!" shouted a husky, butter-colored boy when his tall body whizzed by Carli and me. A pack of older boys ran after him, pushing us into somebody's front yard. We stood there, watching the action just a few feet away.

"FIGHT! FIGHT! FIGHT!" the group of boys trumpeted. Through an open space in a jumble of dark pants legs, I saw fists fly. A slender, brown boy lay on the ground. The husky boy pounded his face like he was punching dough.

Cars neared the scene and slowed up. Their doors clicked locked. But nobody stopped driving. They all rolled on.

"Carli, let's get help!" I whispered.

We backtracked and hurried past the fire station that was next to Hunter. In the school parking lot, I ran up to a stocky, copper-toned man with a thin mustache.

"Mr. Loomis!" I panted. "There's a fight up the street! Right over there! See?!" I pointed at the group of boys bobbing and weaving in a huddle, two blocks away. "This boy's getting beat bad!"

"Well, I can't do nothing about that." I glanced at the Safety Net Security badge pinned to his black jacket. "I got to stay here in the parking lot," he said, folding his arms over his chest, hiding the badge.

"But, he's *hurt!*" Carli said.

"All I can say is go tell them in the office. Maybe they can call the police."

Moments later, in Hunter's office, Carli and I stood in line in front of the desk of a woman so tiny I was probably taller than her—Mrs. Andrews, the school secretary.

"Excuse me, Mrs. Andrews!" I called, peering around the girl at the front of the line. "I don't mean to cut, but there's an emergency!"

"Everybody's got an emergency, honey."

Mrs. Andrews had her dark straight hair pulled into a tight bun. Not bothering to turn her nut-brown face toward me, she pinched the oval rim of her black glasses with two of her miniature fingers. She focused on the navy blue binder that she held open in front of her.

"All these kids need somebody to come pick them up. I'm making phone calls now."

"No—No, I mean *outside*! There's a fight!"

She glanced up. "A fight? Where?"

"Up the street!"

"Fight!" The magic word blazed through the kids that stood in line or sat along the wall. Book bags dropped to the floor and coats fell off laps when kids ditched their places in line or sprung from their chairs. Everybody wanted a look through the office window, a glimpse at whoever was duking it out outside.

"Everybody hush!" warned Mrs. Andrews. "Get back in line! Sit back down!"

"This boy's getting beat up!" said Carli.

"Up the street? Not in the school yard?"

"No. On Bernard. A few blocks away," I answered.

"Well, then that's not... Look honey, I got to call these parents." Mrs. Andrews took her eyes off Carli and me.

My mouth dropped. I couldn't believe it. Didn't she hear what we said? That boy could be getting *killed* right then.

"Who's supposed to pick you up?" Mrs. Andrews asked the girl standing in front of her.

"But can't you call the police?" asked Carli.

"Before that boy gets... before..." I didn't want to think of what came after "before."

Mrs. Andrews sighed real deep. "Okay, honey. I'll call the police."

Now you're talking some sense. Dang!

"Now you two got to move out the way. I got to make phone calls here."

39

I didn't move. I wanted to see her actually call the police. Carli waited next to me.

"Go on now! I told you I'll call. You know you're not supposed to come back in the building when school's out. Not unless you're in an after-school program."

"We had to tell you about the boy—" I said.

"And you *did*. Now you both go on home like you're supposed to."

While Carli and I were leaving the office, I heard Mrs. Andrews on the phone. "They said they're on Bernard. Boys. Probably from the middle school, from Legacy."

Good.

Carli and I walked back through a building that normally seemed bright. I usually thought Hunter's shiny, clear picture windows looked like open mouths bragging about the Honor Roll lists and art projects that showed off on brand new walls. Hunter had gotten rebuilt two years ago. It usually looked fresh. Clean and neat. But today the building seemed just as gloomy as the sunless day, just as gloomy as I felt.

Back on Bernard, Carli and I saw a fire department ambulance parked in front of the spot where the fight had been. We watched two men in dark blue uniforms lift the stretcher that carried a slender, bloodied body into the truck.

"I hope he'll be all right," I said, when I really meant, "I hope he isn't dead."

"Yeah, me too."

CHAPTER 5

SHOWTIME AT THE BEY-ROSS'

Later, my parents and I sat at the dinner table—me in jeans and a red sweatshirt, Mama in an orange sweatsuit, daddy in charcoal grey business pants and a light grey shirt, no tie.

"This boy got beat up on Bernard today."

Daddy sat his fork on his plate with a loud tink. He looked at me like I was from Pluto, not even a real planet.

"What happened?"

"These guys chased him and beat him up."

"Were they from Hunter?" asked Mama. Like Daddy, she had stopped eating.

"Naw. I don't think so. They looked older."

"Where were you while this was going on?"

"I was right there, Daddy. Me and Carli. We were on Bernard."

"I don't like that," Mama said. "Kids fighting in the street. It's dangerous. We need more police."

"We need better parents," said Daddy.

I told my parents how I'd asked Mrs. Andrews to call the police. I told them about the ambulance, too. My news carved worried lines across Daddy's forehead. When he went back to eating, he cut a baked chicken breast into angry little pieces.

Later, I rinsed dirty dishes and put them in the dishwasher. I overheard Mama talking on the cordless telephone in the hallway.

"Marsha, with a Saturday shift I'd be able to pick Taneesha up after school. I just don't like her coming home alone."

Mama's going to pick me up from school?

I knew that tone in my mother's voice. Once she made her mind up, that was it. From now on, I had an after-school ride.

"Yeah. They have an after-school program. Usually she participates. I tried to get her in dance like last year, but the class filled up fast."

43

No more walking up Bernard.

"I can't sign her up for anything else. *All* the activities are full."

No more watching somebody get beat up.

"Miles would do it if he could. But most afternoons he's got appointments when she's getting out of school. So it's on me."

No more feeling scared on the way home.

I was done with the dishes. Standing at the kitchen counter, I dried my hands with a paper towel and thought about how the fight that happened today wasn't the first one I'd seen. But I'd never been so close to a major blowout with older kids before. I'd never seen anybody bloody and beaten, laid out on a stretcher. If I never had to walk home from school again, that would have been fine with me. I smiled to myself at the thought of Mama coming to get me every day.

"I know the staff's tight right now."

Uh, oh. I didn't like the sound of that. Mama's words had sagged.

"Okay. I understand. Sure—"

My poor heart went flat as a birthday balloon a month after the party. Right then, I knew the

deal. I'd still have to walk the ten blocks home—
me and Carli, on our own.

"Well, Marsha, at least you'll have some tem-
porary help next Friday. Taneesha."

Hunh?

"Remember? She's coming in for Take Your
Child To Work Day."

Says who?!

What in the world was my mother saying? I
hadn't talked to her about Take Your Child To
Work Day at all!

Mama walked into the kitchen and clicked the
phone into its cradle on the wall.

"Mama, did you say I'm going to your job for
Take Your Child To Work Day?"

"Yeah. What's up?" With her back to me, she
started pouring powdered detergent into the
dishwasher.

"You didn't talk to *me* about it!"

I was mad as anything over the fact that Mama
didn't seem to think it was important to find out
what I wanted. I stood there steaming because
not only had she not bothered to talk to me about
her peachy plans but she wasn't even taking the
time to look at me right then.

45

"Oh, I'm sorry, sweetheart." She stayed facing back out and pushed the dishwasher door closed. "I have so much on my mind." She turned the dial and the dishwasher whirred softly. "But anyway, it ought to be fun, don't you think?"

Fine time to be asking me what I think.

Trying to keep my temper, I took a real deep breath.

"Mama, I don't want to go." I braced myself for whatever she might say about my big declaration of independence.

And I watched her not even so much as tilt her head my way.

She coolly poured water onto the soil of the potted aloe vera plant in the kitchen windowsill, acting like what I'd said was no big deal.

Unbelievable.

Obviously, my own mother couldn't have given a good tahoot about my feelings.

"But I already made arrangements at Ontario Hospital. When I found out about Take Your Child To Work Day at the PTO meeting." She tossed this last bit of information at me like a scrap to a dog and stooped to place the small

46

plastic watering can she had just used inside the cabinet underneath the kitchen sink.

"But I want to go to school next Friday." My lips tightened. Unlike Mama, I was having trouble staying cool.

"I'm glad you take school so seriously, Taneesha. Really." Crouched low, she fiddled with something inside the cabinet. "But I made sure you could come to the hospital with me."

"But, Mama!"

"Don't be such a worry-wart. It'll be fun. You'll see." She closed the cabinet, stood, and still kept her back to me.

That's it!

"MAMA, YOU'RE NOT LISTENING TO ME!"

She spun around like her feet were greased rollerskates.

"Taneesha, don't you *ever* use that tone with me." Her voice was so unnaturally quiet that it sort of freaked me out. And the look in her eyes was even spookier.

"What's going on in here?" Daddy asked, rushing into the kitchen. He shot a puzzled look at me, then at Mama—who would have had steam blowing out of her ears if she were on the

Cartoon Network. "Taneesha, are you raising your voice to your mother?"

"Daddy, Mama wants me to go to Take Your Child To Work Day!"

"Yeah? I know." He had this little *oh-is-that-all?* tone in his voice. It came with a matching doofus smile. "We figured you'd go to the hospital with your mother this time. Next year, you can come to my office with me."

"You *figured* that, huh?"

He was dissing me just as bad as Mama had.

"When were you going to let *me* in on it?"

They both looked confused. Well, maybe they'd get this:

"Here's some news: I don't want to go!— AND YOU CAN'T FORCE ME!" I stormed out of the kitchen and headed toward the staircase in the living room.

"NOW YOU WAIT ONE MINUTE, YOUNG LADY!"

Daddy's megaphone order stopped me mid-stomp, like one of those giant hooks that pull bad performers offstage in Harlem on TV reruns of *Showtime at the Apollo*. Actually, he sort of scared me.

48

"We just want you to experience a work environment," he said.

Now he was trying to sound all nice and everything. I didn't care. I was still mad.

He gave a big sigh. "Tell you what. Why don't we chant about this? You know what Nichiren said—"

"I don't want to chant."

"Well—" said Mama. I noticed that the fire in her eyes had blown out. "It's time for Gongyo anyway. Come on and sit down. You can lead."

"I don't want to do Gongyo either."

I didn't feel like reciting the evening prayer—Gongyo. I was ticked at my parents for not listening to me. And I knew one sure way to rattle their nerves was to dis Buddhism.

"You need to, Taneesha. You'll feel better," Mama cooed, like she was talking to a baby or something.

It was too late for her to get all coochy-coo, though.

"I don't want to, okay?"

"Listen, Taneesha," Daddy said, back to being mean. "I understand that you're upset—"

You don't understand! How can you?! You're not LIS-TENING TO ME!

That's just what I would have said—and how I would have said it—if they hadn't been bigger than me.

"—but we're a family, a *Buddhist* family. We *pray*. And since you're upset, that's all the more reason to get to the altar. Have a seat."

He gripped the wooden high back of a chair whose seat was covered in moss-green fabric. It was the middle chair of one of three identical ones placed in a row in front of the wooden altar table.

I knew what Daddy's grip on that chair meant: "Sit Down, Or Else." I didn't want to find out what "or else" was so I kept my distance while I waited him out. Refusing to make eye contact with him, I stayed rooted near the stairs to see if he'd press the issue.

Finally, I couldn't bear the heavy pause stuck between me and that mean man. I dragged my feet over to the chair and plunked into it. Those two sat on either side of me.

In the five minutes or so that it took to finish Gongyo, reciting the Lotus Sutra scripture, even though I was supposed to be the leader, I mumbled the words on purpose. I ignored Mama's nagging whispers: "Louder, Taneesha." "Sit up!" "Put your hands together—*please!*" I slouched in my seat and kept my hands limp in my lap throughout the whole dang thing.

They can't make me chant and they can't make me go to crummy old Take Your Child To Work Day, either.

They'll see.

CHAPTER 6

E.T. MEETS
SIX X-RAY EYES

Who are you kidding, Taneesha Bey-Ross? You know you can't do this. You're going to flop!

I did my best to ignore Loudmouth's non-stop jabbering inside my head. Sometimes it took everything I had to tune out Evella's pesky voice poking at me. I hated the way she popped in whenever I was in an uncomfortable situation— like right now, for instance.

This Friday—one week and four days after "Showtime at the Bey-Ross'"—I'd been dragged kicking and screaming (well, griping, at least) into Ontario Hospital for Take Your Child To Work Day.

With my back stiff as my father's jokes, I sat in a brown, pleather-cushioned chair, trying to ignore the fact that my pantyhose felt like Brillo pads. I smushed my knee bones together and kept my beige Payless dress shoes planted on the hard, green floor. Sweat trickled down my chest while I fought the urge to scratch at the itchiness underneath the yellow wool skirt and sweater get-up that my mother had picked out and I *hated*.

Surrounded by walls painted in a blue ocean scene—dolphins, seals, killer whales—three empty chairs were behind me. But my eyes zeroed in on what was in front—the big eyes of three little girls I'd never seen before in my life. They sat across from me in separate beds, wearing pale blue and white striped gowns and ogling me as if I were E.T. the Extra-Terrestrial.

On my lap, I had two books Mama had given me earlier—when she'd introduced me to the girls and then left me all alone in that great big room with them. Thinking of how she had just abandoned me just ticked me off all over again. Why wouldn't it?

In my head, I heard Mama going on and on…

53

"Remember, Taneesha, your evil twin never takes a vacation…"

Plus, Evella played her can't-do noise on top of my brain as if she was stuck on "repeat."

Loser! Loser! Loser!

And I just couldn't control that girl.

Not only that, but knowing that the only reason I had to deal with Evella's blabbermouthing that morning was because Mama and Daddy hadn't *listened* to me had me smoking mad.

Now, I knew my mother's whole evil twin thing was pretty lame. And *weird* when you got right down to it—*split-personality* weird.

Loser! Loser! Loser!

I knew Evella was only imaginary. Just in my head.

Loser! Loser! Loser!

But it really was like I had an evil twin in there.

That's what I was thinking when all of a sudden one little word shined its light in my brain:

Chant.

I was whipped, and right then, that sounded like a real good idea so I started chanting fast in my head.

Those little girls kept looking at me like I was going to say something. But since I couldn't, I just kept chanting in my mind.

I don't know how long we sat like that. Them looking at me. Me looking at them. A minute? Two minutes? I couldn't tell. But I starting thinking something: "Like it or not, Taneesha Bey-Ross, you've got a job to do and there's no way out."

So while those six eyes x-rayed me, I made a decision. Where it came from I couldn't have said.

Loser! Loser! Loser!

But I decided that in spite of Evella's racket, I was not going to let her ruin everything.

At least that was my plan.

"Okay, girls, what should I read first?" I asked, holding up one of the books in my lap. "*Kendra's Not-So-Surprise Party*...or—"

"The party! The party!" squealed a girl, bobbing her chubby body up and down on her mattress. Her two thick braids flapped behind her like floppy wings.

"The Party! Ow!"

"What's wrong, Ebony?!" I stood.

55

"The needle pinched here," she said, pointing to the place where a clear, plastic tube stuck out of her arm.

"Okay. Okay. I...I...I'll get my mother." Panicking, I rushed toward the door.

"No. I'm all right. The needle always do that when I jump on the bed." I looked at her, unsure. "For real. I'm okay."

"Then don't jump on the bed, Ebony. All right?" I eased back to my chair. *Whew! Girl, you nearly gave me a heart attack.*

"All right. But can you please read about the party?"

"Okay." I sat. "I like that one, too."

That wasn't so hard. A little drama, but it's over.

Even though I hadn't wanted to be there at first, I started thinking it would be kind of cool to be able to tell Carli that the little kids at the hospital looked up to me.

I opened one of the books on my lap and started to read: "Kendra couldn't wait. She peeked out from under her red blanket—"

"Nurse Jim read that one yesterday!" A Thumbalina-sized girl sitting on the bed across from Ebony blasted that news. She had short,

56

reddish hair braided in a pattern that looked like the lines on a soccer ball.

"Oh. I didn't know that, Loren. Um…." My mind raced.

See? Told you you'd flop.

I twisted one of my locks and chewed my bottom lip. I tried to think of what to do next. My mother had only given me two books.

Maybe I better go ask her for more.

You are such a *baby!* You can't even get through the first few minutes without Mama!

"Well, I wasn't here yesterday, Loren!" A skinny girl said that. Over a dozen teeny braids were caught in shiny yellow and red baubles that decorated her hair as if it was a gumball garden. "I want to hear about the surprise party, too."

I was glad to know that, thanks to Shantay, the problem was over.

"Okay, girls. I think Shantay's the tie breaker."

"What's that mean?" asked Loren.

"The party wins."

"Goody!" yelped Ebony.

"Aw man!" moaned Loren.

"Sorry, Loren. I'll read the other book next, okay?"

Loren's lip poked out. "Okay."

I started to read again:, "Kendra couldn't wait. She peeked out from under her red blanket—"

"Hey, girls! Sorry for interrupting, but it's time to check your glucose levels."

I looked up.

Mama breezed into the room in dark blue pants and a midnight blue smock that had galaxies glowing and swirling all over it. She carried a tray of medical stuff.

I slumped back in my chair, frustrated. Just when I was getting to work, I had to stop.

"Dang!" said Ebony. "Nurse Alima, we was just getting our story!"

Yeah, dang.

"Hey, Mama," I muttered, waving a blasé hand when she brushed passed me.

She headed toward Loren's bed. "Sorry, girls. I'll be as quick as I can. Taneesha, how're things going in here?"

"Good. Like Ebony said, we were just *about to read*."

I wanted Mama to go away. I was ready to get down to business. With her in the room, I didn't feel so on top of everything anymore.

"Okay. I hear you. I'll be out of your way in a minute. Promise.

"With diabetes we have to make sure glucose levels aren't too high or too low." Mama stood over Loren. "Glucose is sugar, Taneesha. If you've got too much or too little in your blood—"

"You can faint or die," Shantay blurted out, matter-of-factly.

Her words shocked me. The girls seemed fine. I'd almost forgotten they were patients in a hospital. It was hard to imagine that any one of them was really sick.

"Now Shantay," Mama said, fluffing Loren's pillow, "none of you need to worry about that. You're in good hands here. As long as you do what your doctors and parents say, you'll be fine. You just had a few complications—some problems we need to look into—but we're taking good care of you."

I felt better hearing Mama say that. But I also worried about those girls.

I watched Mama hold the end of a thing that looked like a fat white pen without a point to Loren's fingertip. A speck of blood appeared on Loren's finger.

59

Ouch!

I was surprised that little girl didn't shout herself.

"Taneesha, this is a glucose meter. It reads bloodsugar levels."

The new thing Mama held looked like a cell phone without a key pad.

"Oh."

"Okay, Ms. Loren, you just need to take your insulin and you're good to go. Taneesha, insulin helps keep the right amount of glucose in your blood. It also helps your body use sugar correctly."

"Where's it come from?"

"Insulin? Your body makes it. But with Type One diabetes—the kind these girls have—your body *doesn't* make it. So you have to get it from a shot.

"It's also important to eat plenty of fruits and vegetables and move your body every day. But we should do that whether we have diabetes or not, right?"

I rolled my eyes.

Here we go.

"Yes, Officer HP," I groaned, after calling Mama the short version of "Officer Health

60

Police"—the nickname I gave her because some-times she just went too far about health stuff.

Mama laughed a little at the HP thing—and then she stuck a needle in Loren's thigh!

Double ouch!

How come that girl's not screaming?

I paid close attention while Mama went through the same routine with Ebony and Shantay.

"Okay, ladies, you're all set. Breakfast trays'll be coming around in a little while. Enjoy your story. Bye!"

"Bye, Nurse Alima!" said the girls.

"Bye, Mama."

Finally.

I wanted to ask the girls the burning ques-tion that I couldn't ask them with my mother in the room.

"Taneesha—" Mama said, turning back just before she went through the doorway, "later I'll take you on a tour of the hospital. Then you can help me tidy the nurse's station."

"Even *here* I got chores?" I asked, slumping my back against my chair.

"'Fraid so, sweetie." She had the nerve to smile. "Oh, and I'll be bringing by more books in

61

a minute. I meant to give them to you this morning, but things got kind of backed up. Thanks, honey."

"You're welcome," I mumbled.

Like I need extra chores.

My mother passed through the doorway and walked out of sight.

I leaned forward in my chair to ask the girls my scorching question: "Doesn't it hurt to get those shots?"

"A little," shrugged Ebony. "But I'm used to it."

"Yeah, me too. I get 'em three times everyday," said Shantay.

"Only two times for me," said Loren.

Now *that* frightened me. As far as I was concerned, even one shot a *year* was too many.

"Wow. You girls are brave. I hate shots, but you act like it's nothing."

The girls didn't seem so babyish anymore.

Now everything seemed real important. I wanted to make the day extra special for them. I straightened my back and sat taller in my chair.

"Okay, where were we?"

"The party! The party!" squealed Ebony, bobbing up and down on her mattress.

"Watch it, Ebony. Remember?"

"Okay," she said, in mid-bounce. "I'll stop."

"Right. Okay. Here goes."

I opened one of the books on my lap and read: "Kendra couldn't wait. She peeked out from under her red blanket. What surprise would she see?"

I made sure I enunciated the way Mr. Alvarez always told us to do. I said the t's in *couldn't*, *wait*, and *blanket* jusT righT.

Too bad I couldn't have frozen that moment—a moment when everything was okay, not terrible—and thawed it out when I needed it.

CHAPTER 7

No Parents Home

ater, after school hours, Carli and I studied
together as usual. I had changed out of my
scratchy, wool outfit into jeans, a gray
sweatshirt, and my lavender bunny slippers.

My mother had gone back to Ontario after she
dropped me off at home so I could start my
homework. I'd wanted to get going on it and I
couldn't at the hospital because I needed a program that was on my computer.

When Mama and I had pulled into our drive-
way in her dark blue minivan, we'd seen Mr.
Flanagan and Carli sitting in his green car, parked
in front of our house on Rosebush Road, waiting

for us. Like my mother, Carli's father had to go back to work for a few hours after he'd kept Carli with him most of the day.

When Carli and I had taken off our coats in my house that afternoon, I'd noticed that, apparently, she'd gotten to dress down at her father's job instead of itching it up like I did at Ontario. She had on jeans and a beige pullover.

We both liked to finish our weekend homework on Fridays so we could keep Saturdays and Sundays free for whatever. Now we stretched, bellies down, on my living room floor. My locks hung past my face and Carli's red hair hung past hers. She had her left leg, the one with the brace, propped on one of our moss-green couch pillows.

The fireplace and mantle were behind us. In front of us, paper and books sprawled across the softness of the big plum rug, spilled over its edges, and spread over the wooden floor like sugar glaze over a Pop-Tart.

My stomach growled. I was about ready for a snack.

"Hey, Taneesha," Carli said, softly. "Look at the altar."

I looked at it—a large, cherry-wood table with four legs, and, underneath it, a legless, long cubby that was raised on a platform. The cubby had a row of books inside. The altar seemed the same as always.

"So?"

"No, *look*. Don't you see? It's sparkling. It's almost like fairies are dancing on it. Little Tinker Bells."

And then I saw. That Carli, she was right. Today, like every day lately, had been cloudy. But right then, a beam of sunlight shimmied through one of the living room windows and burst into tiny points, dancing on the altar's polished wood.

Light danced on the extras that sat on the altar table, too—on the shiny, red and yellow apples in a terracotta bowl and on the rounded glass of the sea-green water jar. And light danced on the pair of vases that sat on the oval end-tables at each side of the altar—black, glazed vases, shaped like teardrops and holding evergreens that filled the room with their pine smell.

For a silent moment, Carli and I just sat there on the floor, watching the sparkly show.

"What's it all for, Taneesha?" she asked, dreamily.

"What?"

"The things on the altar. What are they for?"

"I've told you that before. Plus they talked about it when you came to meetings."

"Tell me again." Her eyes still followed the lights.

"Everything stands for the five senses plus water is for purity," I sighed, annoyed at Carli for making me rattle off information that she should have remembered already: "Fruit, taste. Beads, touch. Bell, sound. Incense, smell. Candles, sight."

"Your altar doesn't have any candles. Or incense. How come?"

"My parents stopped using candles when I was a baby so I wouldn't start a fire. And my father's allergic to incense. Plus my mother says burning stuff's bad for your lungs."

"Oh."

There was a pause.

"What about the branches?" She was talking about the evergreens Daddy had cut off the tree in our back yard. "What are they for?"

"Leaves stand for forever, for no beginning or end, for how long life lasts."

As irksome as it was to have to answer Carli's twenty-questions, I couldn't help thinking that my parents would have flipped into extreme gush mode if they'd known I was actually telling somebody about Buddhism. Even if it was just her.

"Forever. Hmm. Cool."

We went quiet again.

"I wonder what happened to him," she said.

"Who?"

"That boy from last week, the one who got beat up. I wonder if he's okay."

"Hope so."

"Me too."

More quiet.

"I'm going to chant for him," I said. It seemed like the right thing to do. "Do you mind?"

"No. I'll do it with you."

I stood and reached for the most conspicuous part of the altar, the part Carli hadn't even bothered asking about. Maybe because she remembered what *that* was, even though she'd apparently forgotten everything else she'd ever learned about Buddhism.

I opened the Butsudan, or Buddha's house, the towering, oval cabinet that sat in the center of the altar table, up against the wall. The cabinet that reached toward the ceiling as if it were trying to climb the sky. Then I sat in the middle chair of the three that made a row in front of the altar. Carli sat to my left.

The large altar bell—a shiny, black, bowl-like thing—sat on the floor in the space between Carli and me. The bell was on a purple velvet pillow and the pillow was on a golden pedestal (which was really a big, upside-down brass plant pot).

I took hold of the black wooden handle of the mallet that lay in a wooden cradle on the altar table. With the part of the mallet that was covered in purple velvet, I struck the bell.

While the bell's loud bong faded away, I looked up at the object inside the Butsudan, pressed my hands together, and started chanting Nam Myoho Renge Kyo. Carli did, too. It felt kind of good knowing we were chanting for the same thing. For that boy.

I sent beams of light to him, just like the light that danced on the altar. I imagined him all glowing, not bloody, very safe, and just fine.

After a few minutes, I struck the bell again and Carli and I did Sansho, we chanted three times slowly.

"I hope that helped," she said.

"Me too."

She returned to her spot on the floor and I closed the Butsudan door and followed her. But I didn't start back on my homework right away.

My eyes stayed on the Butsudan. I thought about how I wasn't even tall enough to touch the top of it.

I remembered Mama saying that the rest of the stuff on the altar didn't even have to be there, it was optional. She said that what was *inside* the Butsudan, protected behind closed doors now, was the most important part. I liked to pretend that the tall cabinet was a strong royal guard protecting me, too.

If I had my way, I would never come home to an empty house. But since I almost always do, I imagine that the altar watches over me until my parents get there.

That's a secret, though. I've never told anybody I do that, not even Carli. It's kind of immature.

But if I had known what was coming, while I was all gung-ho on chanting, for every one time I did it for that boy to be safe and protected, I would have done it a thousand times for me.

I heard keys jingling.

I raised my head and glanced over my shoulder through the archway that separated the living room from the kitchen. Mama's face was in the kitchen-door window. I popped up to run and meet her.

A gust of chilly wind blew through the house when she opened the door. She stood on the floor mat, stomping snow from her boots.

"Hey, Mama." I grabbed her around the middle of her frosted black coat and gave her a big hug.

"Hey, little lady." She squeezed me back. "You did a great job today."

I thought so, too. But it felt good to hear her say it.

"Thanks, Mama. You know what? I had a good time. Even the tidying part wasn't that bad."

She laughed a little. "Glad to hear it.

"Hey, Carli!"

"Hi, Ms. Ross!" Carli answered from the living room.

Mama glided through the kitchen, peeling away her black earmuffs, coat, scarf, and midnight blue nurse's smock with glow-in-the-dark galaxies on it; to me, it was her coolest one. She disappeared into the hallway.

I heard water running in the downstairs restroom—Officer HP doing the same wash-your-hands-for-as-long-as-it-takes-to-sing-"Happy-Birthday"-twice routine she bugged me about doing fifty-leven times a day.

Carli and I fixed a snack—popcorn, baby carrots, celery, peanut butter, veggie dip, and hot cocoa. Sitting at the kitchen table with her, I breathed in chocolatey steam. We slurped from mugs, and chomped, crunched, and munched.

"Can you believe it? Next week's the big day already," Carli said, scooping up veggie dip with a carrot.

"What day?"

"Election day, silly."

"Oh. Yeah. Time flies."

The election—the last thing I wanted to think about. Why couldn't I just enjoy my snack and savor the fact that my mother said I'd nailed Take Your Child To Work Day?

"So, before my father comes to take me home, how 'bout I help you with your campaign materials? I picked up some construction paper at the pharmacy in case you need it."

I grabbed a handful of popcorn. "Um... Thanks, Carli. But, naw. I'm good."

"Well... Want me to listen to your speech at least? I can give you feedback."

"No, thanks. I haven't finished editing it yet."

How about, I haven't even written it yet?

"Okay."

She sounded a little disappointed.

So. I didn't ask her to nominate me.

Still, I felt a little uncomfortable about the whole conversation.

"Well," she sighed, "just let me know. You can call me. You can read it over the phone."

"Sure. Maybe I'll do that. Thanks, Carli."

Thanks for *everything*.

"Taneesha, I've got news for you!" Mama called from outside the kitchen.

"Yeah?" I was glad for the chance to talk about something besides the dang election. "What is it?" My words were garbled because I had a mouth full of popcorn.

73

Mama walked into the kitchen and sat at the table.

"What's the news?" I asked.

"Well, I was thinking about how much you really liked meeting the children with diabetes, and how much they liked you, too."

More praise? I like it!

"So, you know my supervisor, Marsha, right?"

"Yeah."

"I asked her if you could come by the hospital after school sometimes to read with the kids. And she said okay. Do you want to do it?"

"Sure! That sounds fun!"

"Yeah, it does," said Carli.

My thrill faded as soon as I saw her face. I could never stand to see that girl looking droopy. I liked the idea of working at the hospital, but it wouldn't have been fun knowing she missed out.

"Mama? Could Carli come, too? I mean, if Mr. Flanagan says it's okay?" I noticed a little smile curling Carli's lips. That made me smile, too.

"You know, I hadn't thought of that. I bet it'll be fine. I just have to ask Marsha to make sure. How's that?"

74

"Fine with me!"

"Me too!" said Carli.

One week and four days ago, who would have believed it? I, Taneesha Bey-Ross, could hardly wait to get back to those little kids at Ontario Hospital—and with Carli at that.

Too bad life couldn't have stayed as sweet as it was right then.

CHAPTER 8

THEY HAD BEEN TO HELL

"Snack time's over, everybody. Please toss your trash in the can."

Gail made that pleasant little request in her pleasant little way. She was the leader of the Elementary School Group, "ESG" for short. Her feathery, blond hair went just past her plump shoulders. And, like me, and a lot of the kids in the ESG room at the Buddhist center my family went to on the southwest side of Cleveland, she had on a sweatshirt, blue jeans, and sneakers. It was Sunday, and it had taken my father about forty minutes to drive to the center from the northeast side of town where we lived.

The ESG room wasn't exactly my favorite spot. But since every first Sunday of the month I had to come to the center with my parents for this World Peace meeting, ESG beat sitting with Mama and Daddy in the Gohonzon room listening to boring speeches and lame music for over an hour. Every once in a while, something fun went on in there, like the African drum and dance group that had played last month, or people would put on a skit or something. But mostly, it was boring.

If it weren't for the snacks I got in the ESG room, I wouldn't have been hanging out there this morning either. I would have hidden in the hallway and ducked into a spare room or the bathroom to stay clear of nosy grown-ups who asked, "Where are your parents, Taneesha?" and, "Why aren't you with the other children, Taneesha?"

Snacks and freedom from big noses was what brought me to those baby meetings where we had to do morning Gongyo, our prayers, super-slow for new kids. When we went that slowly, it was snooze time for me. Sometimes I snored so loudly I woke my own self up.

"Who knows the story of Bodhisattva Never Disparaging from the Lotus Sutra?"

Gail had a way of sounding so chipper it grated on my nerves. My parents said they'd known her since before I was born. All I knew was she could be too much sometimes.

"Ahmed? Can you tell us anything about him?"

"Nichiren wrote about Bodhisattva Never Disparaging in this letter called—"

That was Ahmed for you. I just knew that one day he'd be a professor of Buddhism or something, with his short, football-player-looking self. But right then, he was just annoying, as usual.

Us kids sat on the floor in a circle. The rug we were on was just like the blue-grey indoor-outdoor carpet we had in Room 509 at Hunter. Except it wasn't as new. The ESG room was like 509 in others ways, too. Actually, it was a classroom once. Daddy had told me that the center used to be a one-floor elementary school.

So anyway, there we were, sitting on the floor, all sugared up from granola bars and Hi-C, and Gail and teacher's-pet Ahmed told us about this ancient guy named Bodhisattva Never Disparaging. Gail said people called Never Disparaging names and tried to whop him but he'd run away from their sticks and stones. She said that nutcase would bow and holler back at the people trying to kill him: "I deeply respect you. I won't get mad at you because you have the Buddha nature!"

"They called him Never Disparaging because he never *dissed* anybody," Gail said.

It hurt my ears to hear her trying to sound cool.

She went on and on about how great Never Disparaging was for not getting mad while people were hurling rocks at his block head.

Meanwhile, D'Aja, my best bud at Buddhist meetings, who was about my height but a little heavier, leaned her face so close to mine that I almost sneezed from the shampoo smell of the one fluffy afro puff that stuck up on her head like a black dandelion. She whispered: "If those people were so Buddha'd up, why were they trying to beat the mess out of Never Disparaging?"

"Maybe he got a Buddhaful butt-kickin'!" I whispered back.

D'Aja and I both almost lost it. We managed to keep our giggles to ourselves, though.

I was with her: the Never Disparaging story was stupid. But none of the other kids seemed to mind. Brain-dead, it seemed, from granola bars and Hi-C—too much high-fructose corn syrup.

Hey, Officer HP would be proud of me for saying that, I thought.

Too bad that instead of cracking jokes about Never Disparaging, I didn't take pointers from him on how to duck and run when someone's trying to knock the living daylights out of you.

"Now, guess what?" said Gail. "I've got two surprises! The first one is: We're going to do a skit about Bodhisattva Never Disparaging!" She bubbled like she was doing a commercial for Bodhisattva Never Disparaging running shoes or something. "We'll present it in the large meeting in about an hour!"

"Oh brother," I whispered, rolling my eyes at D'Aja. She rolled hers back.

"Who wants to be Bodhisattva Never Disparaging?" Gail's eyes beamed over the room like blue searchlights.

"I do!" Ahmed jack-in-the-boxed to his feet and shot his hand up past his face, waving it over his slick, black curls.

You'd have thought somebody was going to *pay* him to be Never Disparaging.

"Eager, are we?" I said, and D'Aja and I fell into another secret giggle-fest.

Soon, Gail had divvied up all the roles for the skit. I joined the stick-and-stone throwers. A bit part. That was just fine with me.

"Okay, kids. Before we start practicing our skit, I've got a second surprise: we have a special guest!"

She'd actually clapped her hands when she said that. I felt like I was trapped on *Barney*.

In walked one of my favorite people: Natsuko Hemmings.

"Girls and boys, please say good morning to Natsuko."

We all did. And Natsuko bowed her whole body real low to us and said "Good morning" back.

I sat there looking at Natsuko. She's slim and pretty short. So's her orangey hair. But I figure she dyes it because near her scalp it's black and white. I've noticed that she always wears ankle socks even when she has on a skirt, like the reddish plaid one she was wearing right then. Her skirt didn't really match her black-and-white polka dot sweater or her green rubber snow shoes, but for as long as I've known Natsuko, she's never seemed to care about fashion.

81

I was taller than Natsuko by the time I was eight, even though she's way older than me—probably as old as my grandparents. But when she smiles, and she smiles a lot, like she was doing right then, she looks just like a little girl.

Natsuko is all right. When she catches me hiding out in the hallways at the center, she sneaks me these little hard candies and leaves me alone. She's been doing that since forever. The candies have Japanese writing on the wrappers. They're good.

And she likes to bow. She'll do it when she first sees you, just the way she'd done it when she came in the ESG room. Then she'll do it again to say good-bye.

Thinking about bowing and everything got me onto how I've noticed that a lot of Japanese people like to do it. Take Daisaku Ikeda, for instance, our Buddhist leader, the one my parents call Sensei for "teacher." He bows the same as Natsuko. There he was, right there in a picture on the ESG wall—kind of chubby, in a blue baseball cap, yellow polo shirt, navy blue slacks, and gold-wire-framed glasses—bowing to a bunch of little kids.

I've seen him do it live, too. Well, sort of, on videos in the Gohonzon room, where the altar is

82

huge. I end up there when some nosey grown-up catches me hiding and makes me go sit with my parents. In the videos, Daisaku Ikeda bows at the audience when he walks fast into this auditorium—a Gohonzon room that's way bigger than the one at the community center, a packed house. He's all dressed up then, in a business suit and tie. You can see the grey hairs combed back on his balding head. And he takes off his suit jacket when he sits down at a table to give a speech.

"Natsuko's going to tell us a real story, everybody." Gail was sitting on the carpet with us kids, facing Natsuko.

Sitting cross-legged, lotus-style, I shifted my weight on that flat carpet. My butt hurt but I paid attention anyway. I didn't want to be rude to Natsuko by fidgeting too much.

"Her story's about one of the cruelest things that can happen when we forget to be like Bodhisattva Never Disparaging. It takes place during World War Two."

"I was fourteen when the atomic bomb fell on Japan," said Natsuko, sitting in a chair in front of us kids.

"I lived in a little fishing village not far from Nagasaki. My family caught fish from the ocean. We also had a small rice farm. Because of the war, all the children in our village had to learn how to use spears to stick soldiers if they attacked us. We had to do like this."

Natsuko stood and made her hands hold an invisible spear in front of her chest. She stooped and pushed that spear toward us as if she were sticking a soldier.

She laughed. I laughed. So did D'Aja and some other kids.

"We also had to learn where to run and hide if bombs fall," Natsuko said, sitting again.

"The day the atomic bomb fall on Nagasaki it was very sunny. Sky so clear and blue. No clouds. Salty ocean smell in the air. Like many other days.

"Then everything turned dark. The way it looks just before the sun goes down at night. The dark came from the direction of Nagasaki. Heavy, sticky black rain starts to fall on us. It falls for hours. The rain smells stinky. Like something burning. Turned our clothes and everything it touch black—but my skin did not burn.

"My uncles and aunts and other people from our village left for Nagasaki. To see what happen there. To help. When they got to Nagasaki they saw dead bodies everywhere, burned people everywhere, with peeling skin. People alive in the river. Dead bodies in there, too. My uncles and aunts said those people must have jumped in river to cool off from the burning.

"The people in the river reach out to the ones from my village. They reach out their burned hands and arms. They beg, 'Water! Water!' They cry for help. Their arms looking like they will break if somebody to touch them. The people from my village did not know how to help all those burned ones. They go back home. They tell us what they saw. They say they had been to hell."

After that, everybody stayed real quiet for a long time. Gail, too.

I saw her wipe a tear away.

Then she asked us to say thank you to Natsuko, and we did.

"Natsuko is very fortunate that the black rain that fell on her didn't make her sick," Gail said. "After World War Two ended, many Japanese children and adults, including people who weren't hit by the two atomic bombs that fell on the cities of Nagasaki and Hiroshima, died from the bombs' poison. It gave them cancer.

"Daisaku Ikeda's oldest brother was a soldier in World War Two."

Gail said that when Daisaku Ikeda was a teenager, his brother died in the war. And when a soldier came to tell Daisaku Ikeda's mother what had happened, she turned her back and shook with tears and died a little, too.

Kids started asking Natsuko questions. She answered all of them.

But I had so many questions I couldn't figure out which one to ask first. So I didn't ask any.

CHAPTER 9

SONG OF AN OLD FRIEND

Brrrrrrrrrrrrrrrrrr!" I climbed our back porch stairs behind Daddy. "I'm cold!"

"You should be used to it, girl," said Daddy. He wore his black overcoat and stood at the back door, unlocking it. "The north wind's just blowing off Lake Erie like it does every winter. It makes the air feel colder than the temperature. They call that the 'wind-chill factor'."

"Well, I just call it too dang cold! And dark. I think the sun's bulb blew out. It never shines anymore."

"But it will, honey." Daddy opened the door. "It will."

87

I didn't know about that. Seemed to me, Mr. Sun was on a permanent vacation.

After the World Peace meeting, Daddy and I had spent the day hanging out. We'd gone to Pizza Hut for lunch, the Homestead Buffet for dinner, and watched a movie and walked all over Goldfield mall in between. Mama had been home having what she called "me time."

Daddy and I bustled through the kitchen doorway. Right away we heard Mama:

"Nam Myoho Renge Kyo, Nam Myoho Renge Kyo, Nam Myoho Renge Kyo…"

I could never figure my mother out. She got a whole afternoon to do whatever she wanted and she used it up chanting.

I smelled wood burning and knew she must have had the fireplace going in the living room. I remembered Carli's question on Friday about candles and incense and thought about how Mama was funny like that. Burning that stuff was a no-no but the fireplace was okay. She'd said before that it was because we only use the fireplace sometimes, not every day. But I knew that really it was just Mama not making sense.

I laughed to myself.

"What's funny?"

"Nothing. Just something I remembered."

I stomped snow off my boots while the altar bell bonged three times.

"Hey, Miles? Taneesha? I was waiting for you before doing evening Gongyo. You joining me?"

No, thank you.

I didn't want to join anything but my head to my pillow.

"I'll be right in, dear! Thanks for waiting!"

"I'll pass, Mama!" I hoped my parents wouldn't push it. "It's been a long day! I just want to sleep!"

"That's all right, Taneesha," said Daddy.

Thank goodness.

"Your mother and I can do Gongyo and chant for you. But before you turn in, come read a passage from the Gosho and do Sansho with us."

"Okay."

I figured I could do that with no problem. I wasn't up to doing Gongyo, the whole evening prayer. But I could read a little from the Gosho, Nichiren's writings, and do Sansho, chant three times.

I placed my boots on the shoe shelf in the hallway, hung my coat, hat, and scarf in the closet, and walked into the living room.

A pretty, orange fire blazed in the fireplace, warming the room. Mama sat in the center chair, in front of the altar, in jeans and a blue sweater, and Daddy sat next to her wearing a grey one and black slacks.

"Mama, I'll read something from the Gosho, okay?" I said, ready to throw in "Daddy said I could," if I had to. "And I'll do Sansho. Then I want to go to bed."

"All right, sweetie."

Hey. *That* was easy.

Mama reached underneath the altar table and, from inside the cubby, she pulled the first book from the row of them—*The Writings of Nichiren Daishonin*, the Gosho.

I took the Gosho from Mama, sat next to her, and flipped to a letter I picked a lot to read because it was the first one in the book and short.

"'The Lotus Sutra,'" I read out loud, "explains that the entity of our life, which manifests either good or evil at each moment, is in fact the entity of the Mystic Law.'"

"Now, what does that *mean?*" Daddy asked, raising his left eyebrow. Whenever he did that, he reminded me of Mr. Alvarez, only nicer. Mr. Alvarez's raised eyebrow usually meant he was mad about something.

I read the passage again, slowly, to myself.

Sometimes my parents' little quizzes annoyed me. But I knew that if I didn't just go with the script, I'd probably hear my mother nag: "Come on, Taneesha, just read a little. It's for your own life." I knew that the easiest thing for me to do was just read the book and get it over with. Plus, that evening I thought I understood the passage.

"It means we're always Nam Myoho Renge Kyo, we're Buddhas, no matter if we're acting good or bad."

I hoped that was good enough. I could hardly keep my eyes open. I stretched my arms wide and yawned loud as an elephant.

Daddy laughed a little. "That pretty much says it all."

"Girl, let's do Sansho so you can get to bed."

Who'd a thunk it? Mama was setting me free without even saying, "Just one page of Gongyo."

She struck the altar bell. "Sit up, Taneesha."

Can't help it, can she?

91

I huffed, but I sat straighter anyway.

Mama bonged the bell again and we all chanted together three times.

I stood and kissed her on her forehead. "'Night, Mama."

She kissed my cheek. "'Night sweetie."

I did the same stuff with Daddy and headed for the stairwell.

"Don't forget to set your alarm," he said. "Remember, your mother and I leave early tomorrow."

"I won't forget."

I climbed the stairs. The altar bell bonged. I heard them do Sansho and start Gongyo, their evening prayer. I reached the top of the stairs, entered the hallway, and walked into my room. Their Gongyo begin:

Niji seson

Ju sanmai

Anjo ni ki

Go shari-hotsu...

I closed my door. Too tired to do anything but fall into bed, I pulled the covers up to my neck and turned onto my side. "Sorry Officer HP," I yawned. "I'll brush and floss in the morning."

Muffled words rose up from the living room. I couldn't make them out anymore. A rhythm I'd heard since before I could remember reached my ears like the song of an old friend and rocked me to sleep.

I had no idea that in just a few hours I'd be up against an evil like nothing I'd ever faced before. If I had known what was coming, or who was coming, I would have been downstairs chanting my butt off.

CHAPTER 10

Human-Eating Bigfoot

Monday morning, I slowly opened my eyes. I could just glimpse cloudy daylight seeping through the slats of my window blinds. I rolled my head over on my pillow to check the alarm clock. 8:32 glowed in red light. I blinked my eyes in focus to get a good look at those numbers. They seemed off. Then it hit me: I'd overslept! Daddy and Mama had already left for work. I was supposed to get up and out on my own—and I'd blown it!

I got to Hunter late. In my classroom, I scurried around like a hamster on Mountain Dew. I stripped down to my dress-code black-and-white and put my coat and everything away. Panting, I eased the seat of my black pants into my chair, next to Carli's desk.

"Hey, girl!" she grinned, whispering.

I had nearly fallen a couple of times rushing the whole way to school over chunky snow and slippery ice. Now I was out of breath. I swallowed the last of a toasted-bagel-and-turkey-bacon sandwich. I'd been gobbling it bit by bit since I left home.

"Hey…girl," I said, hoarse.

"Harrumph!" Mr. Alvarez cleared his throat and raised his left eyebrow. Whenever he did that, he reminded me of my father, only meaner. "Taneesha, you're already tardy. You'd do well to stop talking and start your class work."

"Yes, Mr. Alvarez." I slinked down into my seat.

Great. You are SO embarrassing, Taneesha. Why don't you just disappear?

I heard the faint, low dip and rise of Rayshaun Parker and some other kids saying "Ooooooooh."

Pictures of the sheep I saw on last year's field trip to Lake Farm Park flicked through my head. The poor animal stood naked with all its wool shaved off, a weird, hairless thing for all to see.

Guess who's a sheep now? Baaa! Baaa!

I raised my desktop and ducked my head inside, hiding like an ostrich—head in sand, butt in air—totally exposed. I took out my notebook and pencil, closed my desk without even a little *clump*, and read the Problem of the Day off the chalkboard. Then I pressed my pencil on my paper just hard enough to work it without making a sound.

After we finished going over the Problem of the Day, Mr. Alvarez stood in front of us with his arms behind his back. In seconds, forty eyes looked at him and just as many lips were zipped.

"Class, this week's a busy one for us. As you know, this past Friday was Take Your Child To Work Day. Those of you who participated must present a report on your experiences. Presentations begin tomorrow and will conclude Friday."

Just fine. I bet he's going to do alphabetical order like always.

I wished my name began with a Z. Even a P would do. But with Bey-Ross, I always end up being one of the first people picked for alphabetical order. I felt my stomach twisting into a sick knot.

"We are going to give the reports in alphabetical order by last name—"

I knew it!

"But in reverse. Lawrence Young, you will be the first to share your experience with us tomorrow." Lawrence, a scrawny light-skinned boy who looked like a third grader, gave a low groan.

Hunh? All riiiight!

"Questions, anyone? No? Good.

"The other big event we have this week is our class election."

Oh, no!

"Elections take place on Thursday. Tomorrow we'll hear campaign speeches from our candidates for president, vice president, secretary, and treasurer. Candidates, if you want to bring the campaign materials we discussed last week—buttons, posters, flyers, *et cetera*, you can do so tomorrow."

My butt is fried!

I hadn't made one thing for my campaign. I had no idea what to bring tomorrow. Maybe wiry Ronnie Lawson felt the same way. Maybe that was why, right then, his hand flapped like a flag on a windy day over his twelve-inch 'fro. Maybe he was going to confess that, like me, he wasn't ready to give a speech tomorrow.

"Yes, Ronnie?"

"Can we bring food, Mr. Alvarez?"

"Food?"

Food?

"Yeah, you know, to hand out to everybody. I mean, like a snack or something."

Oh brother.

Don't worry. I told you, you'll lose anyway.

"Well. Okay. I suppose a snack will be alright." Mr. Alvarez folded his arms. He made his lips into tight little lines, thinking. Then he said, "We'll just have the speeches and, er, refreshments, after lunch. Sorry your campaigns have to be so rushed, candidates. Between the state tests and our regular work we just ran out of time to get everything in."

Get everything in? I didn't want to get *anything* in. I wanted *out*.

Why does Ronnie always have to overdo stuff?

By the time school ended, life was normal again. To my relief, none of the kids teased me about how Mr. Alvarez dogged me for being late that morning. Even Rayshaun Parker and the rest of the ones who went "Ooooooooh" didn't mention it.

98

Outside, Carli and I walked up Bernard with clouds that hid the sun hanging over us.

Earlier, over lunch, she'd grilled me about my campaign:

"When we get back to 509, can I see your speech?"

"I left it home."

"Did you make buttons?"

"A poster."

"Why so glum?"

"Got a headache."

"How's your head?" Carli asked while we slogged up Bernard.

"Hunh? What do you mean? What are you talking about?"

"Your headache. I'm guessing it's gone, hunh?"

"Oh. Yeah. Yeah, that. I feel a lot better. Thanks for asking."

"So, how long is your speech?"

"Long enough."

"I thought you were going to call me so I could hear it." She sounded kind of down.

"I didn't want to bug you."

I hated lying to Carli, but what was my choice? I didn't have a speech. I didn't even want to be tangled up in any election. But lately, that was all Carli seemed to live and breathe, even though the whole thing was making me sick, including her—the person who'd plopped me knee-deep in this doo-doo in the first place.

"You wouldn't have been bugging me, Taneesha. Don't you know I'm your biggest fan?"

I felt like such a turd.

But the smile on her face was almost enough to make me feel better. Almost.

"FIGHT!"

I jerked my neck to the right. On the other side of Bernard, two girls were at it. One had a face the color of brown sugar. She was maybe taller than my father. And a lot wider than him. She had a bloody cut above one eye. The other girl's lip was bleeding and puffy. She was a little darker than the first girl and about her same size.

The two girls' scratching, pulling, punching, and biting kept up non-stop. Kids barked, "Get her! Get her!" up and down the street. Cars came to a crawl to pass the crowd. Then they picked up speed and zoomed away.

Four blocks from Hunter, the two girls—seventh-graders maybe—were on their own to scratch, pull, punch, and bite until only one was left standing.

"Hey, you! White girl! What's up with your leg? Is it broke?"

The shout had come from somebody on my side of the street. It grabbed me by the ears and whirled me around.

Say it isn't so.

I saw none other than big bad Shrek herself, in all her raging-red-jacket glory, standing over Carli.

I noticed Carli lying on her butt on the sidewalk. Apparently, she'd slipped on the ice. I helped her to her feet. We stood side by side.

Carli brushed snow off her coat. "No, my leg's not broken. It got hurt when I was a baby, but I'm okay now. I just have to wear a brace to help me walk."

"What you mean you got to wear a brace to help you walk? You mean you a *cripple*, right?" The older girl pointed to Carli's leg. She sprayed nasty laughter into the cold, winter air. "Hey, you ain't nothing but a little cripple, *white girl!*"

101

What is she doing?!

"I am not a cripple! I just wear a brace, that's all!"

I couldn't hear what Carli said after that because that older girl's devil laugh strangled her words.

I got so mad, I couldn't see. "You leave her alone!" I felt my heart bursting out my chest. "She hasn't done anything to you! You're being mean and stupid!"

I froze, wanting to say, "Why are you doing this? Why are you being so mean?"

But I couldn't.

Because just then I saw something that totally ghostified me.

Pure viciousness.

It burned in the eyes that looked back at me. For the first time, I really noticed that girl's size. How she towered over me, not like an irritable-but-harmless Shrek on PMS, but like a Sasquatch, a ferocious, human-eating Bigfoot.

You better back off, Taneesha. This girl can hurt you for real.

Carli gently took my hand. "Let's just go home, Taneesha. It's okay. I'm all right."

"Oh yeah?" growled Bigfoot. "Well, I don't

102

like the way *your* friend here just spoke to me, little *cripple girl*."

That *does* it!

"She is *not* a cripple," I said, through clenched teeth. "She has a *name*. You shouldn't call people ugly names! You wouldn't like it if somebody called *you* one!"

"Is that right? Well, what *you* going to do about it?" That girl was so close, I smelled chiliburger on her breath. And worse, she looked ready to pounce.

As cold as it was outside, sweat started dripping down my forehead. I didn't know what to do.

Run, scaredy-cat, RUN!

I wasn't stupid. I would have run if my feet hadn't been sticking to the ground like they were screwed there.

I looked up at the girl and made my eyes real wide. I bet I looked dumb.

"I-I-I was just s-s-saying that you didn't need to be mean. Th-th-that's all." And I sounded dumb.

On top of that, all of a sudden, I had to pee real bad. That's all I needed, to pee myself in front of a crazy girl that looked like she could kill me—and would.

"Well, I think you need to M-Y-O-B! Mind your own *bizzzzzz-nesss*. Hear me?" On the last two words, she poked her finger at my nose, just missing it.

I backed up and I ducked my head, hating being such a coward, especially in front of Carli.

"Yes."

"What you say?!"

"I said, 'yes.' I hear you. I'll mind my own business."

"Good," she grunted through a twisty smile. "Don't worry. I'm going to make sure you keep your promise!"

She swiveled around and headed down Bernard.

After a minute, Carli and I started up the street again.

"Carli, let's not tell our parents, okay?" I said, quietly.

"What?! But don't you think they should know what happened?"

I didn't want to hear my parents telling me to chant. I didn't want to hear anything from the Gosho either. I'd almost gotten beat up, and tacking one of Nichiren's quotes on that fact wasn't going to make it all better.

104

"I'll handle it, okay? Promise you won't tell?"

"All right," Carli said, all like I-don't-know-if-this-is-a-good-idea. "I promise. I won't tell."

CHAPTER 11

FLOUNCING OUT

At my house, Carli and I sat at the kitchen table. In silence, we drank soymilk and snacked on crackers, tuna salad, and cucumbers.

"So, Taneesha, can I read your speech, now?" Carli asked in a voice that wasn't as zippity as it normally was when she got on that subject.

I didn't want to hear anything about the stupid election. I wished I could wave a magic wand and erase everything that had happened today.

"Did you print it out yet?"

"No, Carli. You *cannot* read my dang speech and I wish you'd have kept your mouth shut and not nominated me at all."

106

She hung her head.

"Oh. I didn't know you felt that way. Sorry."

Hot blood rushed to my face. I wanted to snatch back my witchy words and unsay them.

Can't you do *anything* right, Taneesha?

I reached across the table and patted Carli's hand. "I'm sorry, Carli. It's not your fault. I'm just—I'm just scared, that's all."

"About the election?"

"No! I mean, yes—but that's not all. That girl. She was mean. What if she comes back tomorrow?"

"Well, maybe she won't."

"But you heard her. She said she was going to make sure I mind my own business. Maybe she's even planning to do something to you. Haven't you thought about that?"

"I think we should tell our parents, Taneesha. It's crazy not to."

"I don't want to, Carli. Don't tell, okay? Let's just see how things go tomorrow first? Please?"

"I think you're making a mistake. Sometimes you need help and this is definitely looking like one of those times to me."

"Please, Carli?" I hated begging, but I couldn't

stand the idea of my parents finding out what happened.

"Okay. I won't tell. At least not before tomorrow. After that, I'm not promising what I'll do."

"Okay. That's fair. Thanks."

"Thanks" wasn't a big enough word for how I felt about Carli right then. Sure, she'd really messed me up with the whole nomination thing, but saving me from whatever know-it-all advice my parents would dump on me if they knew about the older girl almost made up for it. I'd been dumped on enough for one day. I didn't need my parents adding to the pile.

By the time Carli and I finished our homework, Mama was home. While she made dinner, we worked on a campaign poster in the living room. I'd had to confess to Carli that when I told her I'd made a poster, I'd really meant, "I have a board that'll work for poster."

I used a purple marker on a giant, yellow-but-used-to-be-white poster board I'd dragged up from the basement. It smelled musty, like dragon breath, and had **COLOSSAL YARD SALE** in huge, red letters on its bad side and lots of black

108

mildew dots on its "good" side. But it was all I had, so it went with it.

I magic-markered this on it in big letters:

TANEESHA 4 PRESIDENT

Carli and I drew a bunch of colorful flowers all around the slogan for decoration. I tried to make the mildew dots look like pollen springing from the flowers but the more I looked at my artwork, the more I had to admit that my idea had tanked.

Whatever.

Once I was done, I propped the poster against the moss-green couch.

"That looks okay," I said, real dry.

"Want to make buttons or something? I brought the construction paper in case you needed it."

"Naw. I think the sign's enough. I don't want to overdo it."

I didn't care about the dumb campaign. It took every bit of my energy to make that poster.

All I could think about was the older girl, Sasquatch, about how angry she'd looked when she said "M-Y-O-B!" Her booming voice filled every space in my brain like an endless lion's roar. In my mind, I could see that ferocious beast—a big brown lion in a puffy red coat, tearing into me with her fangs. And, when she finished, leaving me on the ground—a heap of brown noodles with blood-red sauce.

A while after Mr. Flanagan had come by to drive Carli home, my parents and I sat at the dinner table.

"Taneesha, I spoke to Marsha," said Mama, all teeth. "My supervisor. She said you and Carli can start coming to the hospital on Friday afternoons to read to the children. How's that sound?"

"Fine."

I stared at the food on my plate.

"I called Carli's father this afternoon and told him about it. You two can start this Friday."

I could hardly hear Mama. Only the sound of Sasquatch the Bigfoot's lion's roar: "M-Y-O-B!" I knew that was two different creatures mixed together—Sasquatch/Bigfoot and a lion—but I heard it anyway. I just knew I was fixing to be that ugly creature's meal.

"You remember Shantay, right? The little girl? I told her, too. She's all excited."

I didn't move, blink, or speak.

I wished Mama would stop talking. Her voice was scratching at my brain like sandpaper. Add that to the big beast howling in my head and it was enough to make a girl go crazy.

"Are you all right?" she asked.

"Yeah, Mama. I'm fine."

"You sure, honey? You're mighty quiet today. I thought you'd be happy about this news. Last week you were so excited about Carli coming with you to the hospital."

"I said I'm okay, Mama. All right?"

"Taneesha, watch your tone with your mother," warned Daddy, mid-chew.

"I'm done now anyway."

I scooted back, stood, and grabbed my plate off the table. The food looked gross.

"Wait, don't throw that out—" began Mama.

Too late.

My uneaten dinner—a grilled salmon filet, brown rice and steamed broccoli, carrots and cauliflower—slid into the garbage pail.

"Girl, do you know how much salmon costs?!"

You'd have thought I'd just thrown *her* into the garbage.

I felt a twinge of guilt. I thought of the bony, starving kids that she always told me about when I threw away food. But the guilt passed. I just wanted to get out of there.

"Sorry," I said, not meaning it. "I got to study."

I flounced out of the kitchen. I knew I'd flounced because I felt my parents' eyes drilling into my back and looking at me all like "Why are you flouncing out on us?"

I walked through the living room and caught sight of the altar. I stopped. I thought about the practice, about all the times I'd chanted with my parents but hadn't really wanted to. I thought about how I'd only done it because they'd made me.

I'd chanted at meetings but I was always glad when I could escape. The only times I'd practiced on my own were when I wanted something real bad—like not getting nominated for class president. Now *that* had worked out real well, hadn't it?

But sometimes Nam Myoho Renge Kyo came through. Like when I chanted at the hospital Friday. But then again, I could have done the same thing without chanting. All I had to do was read to some little kids. That was nothing when you got right down to it.

But what about my bike? My magenta ten-speed from Summit Cycles? Mama and Daddy were all set to buy me a $35 used bike from Mr. Garrett, the bike man down the street. But I chanted for the ten-speed I'd seen in the window at Summit Cycles. And the bike shop ended up putting the last one, the floor model, on sale for *exactly* $35. I got it for my birthday. No getting around that, I chanted me up a new bike. A nice one, too.

But even for stuff I'd really wanted, like my bike, I'd never chanted more than a few minutes. Thirty minutes max to be exact. That was for Disney World. Before the trip, Mama had told me I had to chant a half hour every day for a whole month in order to go and, as usual, Daddy backed her up.

I had hated being forced like that. I just knew that making your kid chant had to be against some kind of Buddhist rule or something, or should have been.

I paid my parents back by chanting in a tiny whisper for the whole month. I said my throat hurt.

But I'd gotten to go to Disney World last summer. That was pretty cool. Only talk about *hot*!

CHAPTER 12

DOWNRIGHT DANGEROUS FLORIDA

Standing in the living room, I started thinking about Florida. Before we went to Disney World, we spent four days at this Buddhist retreat in the Everglades—the Florida Wildlife Buddhist Center, the FWBC. That hadn't been half bad.

We'd had our own rooms in one of these one-floor buildings called dormitories. They were covered with stucco like a lot of the houses and buildings down there were. My room was connected to Mama and Daddy's, but I closed my door whenever I wanted to.

The food was great. We ate in this big cafeteria.

I had lobster for the first time, on pizza at that.

At night, we heard alligators croaking in the lake. They were going "Croak! Croak!" It was really spooky. But cool, too. The people that ran the FWBC said the bank on the edges of the lake was too high for the alligators to climb out. I didn't care, though—I wasn't taking chances. I stayed away from that lake like those people told us to.

I stayed out of the grass, too—with its big, fat, green blades—so fire ants wouldn't get me. The name of those ants alone told you what they were all about.

The more I thought about it, the more I realized that Florida was downright dangerous. But it hadn't seemed like it at the time. What had seemed more dangerous was the possibility that I'd make an all-out fool of myself in front of a bunch of people I'd just met. And, thanks to my mother, I got my chance.

Still, there was no getting around it, Florida was beautiful. In the daytime, you saw sky so blue it looked like a painting, not the real thing. And, just like on postcards, palm trees danced in the breeze everywhere.

Now, I'd realized this before, I wasn't a natural mingler. But something about Florida made me mingle. I made friends with kids from all over the country—from California, Atlanta, Minnesota, Texas, New York. You name it. Jocelyn and Dennis, a sister and brother, even came from England with their mother. And this other girl, Akiko, her parents brought her there from Australia.

And there were these bikes that we got to ride around the campus. That's what they called the place where the FWBC was, "the campus," just like at a college. But, of course, none of those bikes compared to my magenta ten-speed. Now, seriously, how could they?

They had ESG meetings there, too. I should have known they would. But I didn't mind them so much. To tell the truth, they were kind of fun.

In ESG, we got to choose different activities. I had a hard time deciding between two of them: circus stuff and Kung Fu. In the end, I went with the clown.

She taught everybody tricks. She said clowns use Buddhism all the time, or something like that. All I knew was I learned how to juggle four oranges. I could still do it.

On our last day at the FWBC, we had a big talent show in the cafeteria, kids and grown-ups together. I read one of Daisaku Ikeda's poems. I knew the poem already because I'd read it in a book Gail, the ESG leader here in Cleveland, had given me a while back.

In the living room, I walked over to the altar and sat in the middle chair in front of it. In the row of books inside the altar's cubby, I saw my book—*Fighting for Peace: Poems by Daisaku Ikeda*. I pulled it out, started flipping through it, and remembered the day I stood on stage in the FWBC cafeteria, in purple shorts, sandals, and ashy legs, and read in front of all those people.

At first, I hadn't known what to do for the FWBC talent show and I hadn't planned on being in it anyway. And, of course, Evella wouldn't have been her self if she didn't have a bunch of really good reasons why being in the show was a bad idea.

What if you stutter? What if people laugh at you? What if a hurricane blows through while you're standing up there on that stage, Taneesha? You should be checking out places to run for cover, not humiliating yourself in front of *strangers!*

But a lot of kids were doing it, being in the show. Even ones who were way more shy than me. So I'd started thinking maybe I might be in it, too. Only, when I got that brilliant idea, I didn't have a talent.

Then, in the FWBC bookstore, I saw Daisaku Ikeda's book and I remembered this poem I'd read in it once. The bookstore people let me photocopy it.

I didn't read the whole thing for the show. I skipped some parts at the beginning and lots of the middle. Daddy had said that might be a good idea since it was real long. I used one of the computers at the FWBC to type up just the parts I was going to read.

In the living room now, sitting in front of the altar, I found, tucked inside my book, the crinkly white sheet of paper with my poem typed on it. I was still irritated with my parents and I didn't want to give them a reason to celebrate—"Taneesha's reading Sensei's poem!" I could just hear them. And I didn't want to. So I read the poem very quietly:

Long have I walked
the roads of this world,
leaving behind
so many memories,
creating so much history.

I have no regrets.
For in my justice-loving heart
has burned the flame
of compassionate determination
to rid the world
of fear and war...

I have forged
a broad, new path of peace.
With the passion of my youth,
with brightly burning eyes,
I sought to create
an ideal world
such as people have dreamed of...

...World peace.
Nothing remains to me,
I have no other wish,
than the realization
of this dream...

120

There have been
bright and beautiful
seasons of spring.
There have been days
when the closing fog
obscured everything.
These memories
are already part
of the distant past,
and yet they are the source
of an energy that is
deep and powerful
and wondrous...

History is in
ceaseless motion.
And with it the people's
wisdom and discernment grow.
Do not overlook the fact
that with every passing day
they stretch their wings
and stroke through the air
with ever greater wisdom.

Ringleaders of violent turmoil
plunging all
into the deepest pits of misery,
leaving them
weeping there!

"Evil leaders depart!"
This is the cry
of all people everywhere.

Our desire is to walk
with our intimate friends
beneath the cherries' full bloom,
inhaling the fragrance of peace,
caressed by warm breezes
and sharing our hopes
in pleasant conversation.

Strike the bell signaling
the arrival of peace!
Firmly sound the resonant chimes
announcing peace,
announcing victory
to people everywhere.
From a dark and blackened sun

raise your sights,
and regard the brilliant
sun of peace!

Holding the book and crinkly sheet of paper on my lap in the living room, I remembered how, at the FWBC, as soon as I'd finished reading onstage, everybody had started hooting and hollering. They even got out of their seats, clapping for me, giving me a standing O. It had been amazing. My stomach had done all these flip-flops, but in a good way.

Then I'd looked down, and, unbelievably, saw my mother crying right in front of me. It wasn't like a real theater, where the audience is in the dark; in that screaming-bright cafeteria, I couldn't miss her.

She sat next to Daddy, with tears streaming down her face, dabbing her eyes with this raggedy ball of Kleenex that she'd dug up from the bottom of her junky purse. I *saw* her dig it up.

She wasn't crying out loud, or anything, only silently. But *still.* Talk about embarrassing. I'd thought I'd die right up there on stage.

Later that night, while my parents and I biked

back to our dormitory, I'd looked ahead at the place where the tops of palm trees touched the night sky and seen zillions of stars twinkling up there. More than I ever saw in North Cleveland. And my parents had said they were proud of how I'd read that poem. They said Daisaku Ikeda would have been proud of me, too.

"Sensei had the FWBC built for us," Daddy had said, pedaling next to me. "And he's had schools built in different countries, too. From kindergartens to colleges. Even a university in California."

"I know, Daddy. You told me that before."

"It's not just for Buddhists either. It's for everybody."

"I know, Daddy. You told me."

Mama, who was riding on the other side of me, had started humming a little song. I'd figured it was a signal for Daddy to change the subject. He must have picked up on it because he went mute.

I've had the feeling for a while that when it's time for college, my parents want me to go to that university Daddy was talking about. The one Daisaku Ikeda built. Do I want to go? I don't know.

Sitting in the living room at that very moment, I was just trying to figure out how to live through fifth grade.

I sighed, closed the book, and sat it on the chair next to me.

I felt myself smiling—it almost felt strange for my face to get into that position.

I sighed again. "Good old Florida."

I had to admit, it was kind of all right meeting so many kids that chant. Only a few kids at Hunter do it. And none of their parents go to meetings as much as mine, or hold meetings at their houses a few times a month like us. But at the FWBC, I was just like everybody else.

"Okay, Taneesha," I whispered, "sitting here strolling down memory lane and everything is nice but you've got to get back to reality."

My life was on the line after all.

I knew sometimes my parents could chant for over an hour. Even as long as two hours. Or more. To me, chanting that long seemed like it had to be torture. But if it could keep me from getting my teeth knocked out tomorrow, I figured, why not give it a try?

I stood, walked over to the light switch on the

125

wall, and flipped it. A warm spotlight from the ceiling flickered on and lit the center of the oval altar cabinet, the Butsudan.

I opened the Butsudan's doors, sat in the middle chair in front of the altar, and scooted forward. I pulled open the large altar table's slender drawer and took out my string of prayer beads. I struck the bell with the mallet. Its bong echoed through the room.

Wait.

Without looking around, I felt Mama standing next to me. The arm of her fuzzy, pink sweater came into view. I whiffed up the aroma of the bowl of oranges she placed on the altar table.

She leaned into my face and smiled.

I didn't smile back.

I wanted her to leave me alone so I wouldn't have to listen to a load of instructions.

Her footsteps padded across the carpet. I heard her messing with the logs in the fireplace, moving them around with the long, black iron tongs.

I waited.

No way was I chanting with her in the room.

In a few minutes, I smelled burning wood and

heard it crackling. The fire's orange glow reflected off the altar and I began to feel warm.

Her footsteps left the room.

Good.

I placed my string of lavender plastic prayer beads over my middle fingers and pressed them between my palms for prayer. Five shorter sections of beads extended from the long, main loop like a stretched out neck and pairs of arms and legs. Each one of the five sections of beads had a fuzzy, white cloth ball attached to its end. The fuzzy balls were like a head, hands, and feet. The "feet" (two balls) dangled from the back of my left hand and the "head" and "hands" (three balls) dangled from my right.

I felt the smooth roundness of the little plastic beads between my palms. And I remembered Gail saying that the string of beads looked like a person when you held it up by its "head." She said holding prayer beads reminded us that we hold our own lives in our hands.

With my hands pressed together in front of my chest, I kept my back straight, and looked upward. My eyes focused on what hung on a little wooden hook inside the Butsudan—a scroll, more than a foot long, made of silky, olive-green cloth and cream-colored paper. The green cloth framed the paper. The paper had bold, black, Chinese letters written on it; it was my family's Gohonzon.

At the altar, my eyes took in the Chinese letters that flow, like a dancing, black river, down the middle of the Gohonzon. I can't read the letters but I know they spell "Namu Myoho Renge Kyo," and I know that means, "I devote my life to the Wonderful Law of the Lotus Flower Teaching of the Buddha."

Don't ask me how I know that mouthful; I just do.

For a moment, I just sat there, with my palms pressed together, staring at the writing on the Gohonzon, thinking. I thought about how Mama says, "Nam Myoho Renge Kyo is your life itself, Taneesha." And that if I chant to the Gohonzon, I can see that I'm a Buddha—that life, my life, never goes away, that I'm everything and everyone and everywhere, all the time. "The Gohonzon is a mirror," Mama says, "a mirror for seeing you."

"Well, then," I whispered, "let's see what I can see."

128

I did Sansho, chanted three times slowly; then sped up. I tried to chant like a galloping horse the way I remembered somebody saying you should do, maybe Gail. I tried to feel that—the freedom of a horse galloping toward a sunny horizon.

But it was no use.

I didn't feel one bit free or sunny. I was a slave, chained to the runaway thoughts in my head.

My mouth said "Nam Myoho Renge Kyo" all right. But my mind spun out of control and Evella did her best to take over:

My face won't get smashed in. I won't get a broken nose—or arm. I will not wish I had signed up for Kung Fu instead of the clown at the FWBC.

But you *should* have. Because Bigfoot's going to *pulverize* you!

Why'd she have to pick on Carli anyway? Why does she want to beat me up? I didn't do anything to her...

Except you called her mean and stupid—*that* was smart!

But she *was* mean and stupid! And big…
Shoot! I'm scared. Really, really scared.

You *should* be. You' re going to get *smacked down*!

I bonged the bell and did Sansho to finish.
"So much for that."
I felt worse than I did before I sat down.

CHAPTER 13

GAGGING UP GUAVA-MANGO JUICE

"Vote for me and I'll set you free! R-O—DOUBLE-N—I-E!"

On Tuesday afternoon, I slowly munched on a chocolate-chip cookie and watched in horror. I couldn't believe it. Ronnie Lawson twirled on his back, making dizzying circles on the floor for the big finish of his campaign rap. Hiphop drumbeats blasted from a humungous old-school boombox—a contraption Ronnie had lugged into the classroom that morning. Kids, including Carli—who claimed to be my "biggest fan," not Ronnie's—were on their feet, dancing, clapping their hands, and snapping their fingers. And Mr. Alvarez didn't even mind.

I was the only one in my seat, fiddling with a neon orange glow-in-the-dark **VOTE•RONNIE** pencil. It sat on my desk next to a paper cup of some of the best juice I'd ever tasted. It wasn't regular old orange or apple juice either. It was guava-mango. Ronnie said his aunt from Jamaica made it. The cookies and pencil came from him, too. Cookies. Pencils. Juice. Bribes Ronnie Lawson passed out to the whole class.

I watched him bow and strut a cool victory dance. Kids shouted "Whooooop! Whooooop! Ronnie! Ronnnie!" and gave him an endless standing ovation.

Still sitting, I twisted the end of one my locks.

"Well, Ronnie!" beamed Mr. Alvarez after the hoots and hollers died down. "I see you really put a lot of effort into your campaign. Nice job."

"Thank you, Mr. Alvarez. I take serving my fellow students seriously, you know. A leader got to do that."

"Yes. Yes. That's true. Very true."

A smilier-than-ever Mr. Alvarez turned to everyone, and said, "Okay, Room 509, calm down, now. Please take your seats. We've seen all the candidates but one."

I hoped against hope he wouldn't say—

"Taneesha, your speech, please."

I sighed, feeling the entire universe on my shoulders. I reached under my desk, and pulled out my rolled up poster.

Don't do this, Taneesha. Why don't you say you're sick? Didn't you see Ronnie's speech? He had *guava-mango* juice for goodness sake! *AND A SHOW!* You're just going to look dumb!

I rubbed my sweaty palms on my blue slacks and started rolling the rubber bands off the poster.

One. By. One.

"Come on, Taneesha," said Mr. Alvarez, back to his unsmiley self. "We have other things to do this afternoon than watch you turtle along."

Rayshaun snickered.

Some other kids said, "Ooooooooh."

And I felt lower than a turtle's belly—I could thank Mr. Alvarez for sticking that image to my brain.

With bent shoulders, I walked the plank from my desk to the front of the room.

"Who pooted?" someone whispered.

More snickering.

At the chalkboard, I faced the class and held the smelly, monster-size poster in front of me. It covered my whole body except for my forehead and below my knees. I couldn't see anything but the back of that thing. The bottom line of the last fat, red L in **COLOSSAL** bumped against my nose.

"Vote for me, please."

"Taneesha, speak up. I'm sure no one heard you."

I took a deep breath. The poster's funk almost made me sneeze but I stopped myself.

"I said, 'Vote for me, please.'"

"That's better. I guess."

So.

I didn't want to be president anyway.

I waited. No one said anything. I waited some more. I began to creep back to my seat.

"Taneesha? Is that it?"

"Yes."

"Oh…*kay-eee.* Class…It seems we should give Taneesha a hand."

Soggy claps hit my ears like wet, drippy socks. Or rotten tomatoes.

I officially wanted to turn invisible forever.

"Your speech wasn't so bad," Carli said later, as we walked up Bernard after school under an overcast sky—the perfect kind for a lousy day.

"Get real, Carli."

You were whooping it up to Ronnie's rap just like everybody else.

"I know my speech stank."

Everybody knew it stank. I planned to stuff my reeking poster in the garbage as soon as I got home.

"Well...so...it doesn't have to."

"What do you mean?"

"The election's not until Thursday. You can bring in something tomorrow. You can make a better speech. I bet Mr. Alvarez will let you try again."

Carli had a point. So I really didn't want to be class president. That didn't mean I had to run a wimpy race.

"Will you help me?"

"Do you have to ask?"

We giggled.

"What's so funny?"

My heart stopped cold.

I would have recognized that voice anywhere.

A hard poke on my shoulder from behind pushed me forward. I caught my balance to keep from falling and turned around.

"I *said*, what's so funny? What's the joke?"

The older girl glared down at me.

"I... I... I wasn't laughing."

What was my mouth doing?

Why don't I just drop dead right here?

"Yes you was laughing. I heard you. What's the joke? You *better* tell me."

"I don't remember."

A volcano erupted in my stomach. I knew that nothing I said would be good enough for that girl.

"You *lying!*" She pulled her fist back. "Tell me or I'm going to pound your face in."

"She's going to help me with my homework!" I blurted. "I was happy about that. That's all!"

"Oh, so you stupid, hunh? You need your little cripple friend's help. I should have known it was something like that.

"Next time I ask you a question, you answer me. You better not lie to me again. Got it?"

"Yes."

136

"That's right."

She turned sharp on the thick heels of her black army boots, the way soldiers do, and started down Bernard.

I gagged up guava-mango juice and gulped it back down.

"My promise is over, Taneesha!" whispered Carli. "I'm telling my father. You should tell your parents, too!"

"Carli, don't!"

"I *have* too. That girl can't just keep bullying you."

It seemed every possible, horrible thing was crashing down on me at once. I couldn't just let Carli take away the only little control I had left. I wanted to decide how, or even if, I'd tell my parents what was happening. Carli had no right to butt her big nose in it—*she* wasn't the one getting bullied. I was.

"Well, you don't have to worry about it!" I screamed. "That girl's not doing anything to *you*, is she? So just stay out of it, Carli Flanagan! That's what you're doing anyway! Staying out of it! YOU'RE NOT DOING *ANYTHING* TO HELP!"

I didn't care how hurt Carli looked. I ran off, leaving her behind me. I didn't look back, even though I knew she could never catch up.

CHAPTER 14

THE MEAN LAUGH

Who made me Carli's bodyguard any-way?" I huffed and hoofed it up Bernard. "I'm just a kid!" Huff, huff. "Who's bodyguarding me?" Huff, huff. "Hunh? No-frigging-body!" Huff. "That's who!" My feet crashed down onto the sidewalk, one after the other, breaking through clumps of snow and ice.

"Ever since first grade I've been Carli Flanagan's official Shoten Zenjin!" Huff. "Her *protector!*" Huff. Huff. "Well, *I'm sick of it!*" Huff. "I QUIT!"

"LEAVE ME ALONE!" Carli's first-grade face was invading my memory and I didn't care who heard me yelling at it. "Go on and look scared!" Huff. Huff. "I don't want this job anymore!" Huff. "GO A-WAY!" But Carli's frightened little six-year-old mug stayed put in my head, right between me and Aristotle Avenue, which was only four blocks away.

My mind flashed back to when I first met Carli.

"What's wrong with her?" said a light-skinned boy with sandy hair: Rayshaun Parker.

"Look! She white," said a girl whose name I didn't know.

"Why she walking like that?"

I didn't see who said that.

I couldn't keep up with who was speaking anymore because it seemed like every mouth was running, whispering about the redheaded girl who had just walked into Mrs. Boyd's first-grade classroom.

All us kids were sitting at our desks. Our new teacher, Mrs. Boyd, had told us to stay in our seats. She was wearing a sky blue skirt and a buttoned-up jacket that matched it. Her straightened hair, which hung past her shoulders, was dark and curly with orange streaks. I thought she was pretty.

Us kids all had on dress-code blue, black, and white, me included. I had on black pants.

The girl who stood just inside the doorway wore a dress, a dark blue one, with a light blue shirt under it. And she had on black shiny shoes and white tights. Even on the leg with that metal thing on it.

It was the first day of school. Everybody was whispering about the girl at the door. Everybody but me. I watched her, though. I knew the look on her face. She was scared.

It sounded like somebody had opened a jar of bumblebees in the room.

"Girls and boys, settle down, please! We have one more student joining us."

The bees kept buzzing.

"In Mrs. Boyd's room, *every* child is welcome. If you don't learn any other rule this year, you will learn that."

The lid clamped down on the jar of bees.

"Thank you. I'm glad you have *that* much sense." Mrs. Boyd beamed her eyes at each boy and girl in the room including me and I hadn't even been buzzing.

"Girls and boys, this is Carli Flanagan.

141

Everyone please politely say, 'Good Morning, Carli.'"

"Good Morning, Carli!"

I watched the new girl's face. It turned so red it looked like she was painted. The red in her face almost matched the red of the wavy hair that fell down her back. The red in her face almost made it so you couldn't see all the little brown dots on her cheeks. But you could still see them, though.

I thought I knew why that girl looked so red. I bet it wasn't just from being late to school either. Like me, I bet she'd heard the mean laugh inside some kids' words. They had said "good morning." But not everybody said it politely like Mrs. Boyd had told them to.

At lunchtime, kids talked loud in the crowded lunchroom. I put my green plastic tray on a long, light brown table and sat next to Carli Flanagan. That was easy since the other kids at the table didn't sit in any of the seats around that girl.

I could see those kids looking at her, though. A few seats away from her and across the table. They put their hands over each other's ears and whispered. They pointed their fingers.

"Hi, Carli," I said. "I'm Taneesha."

My tray had a tossed salad, two slices of cheese pizza, and an apple juice box on it.

"Hi, Taneesha."

I saw the same stuff on Carli Flanagan's tray as mine.

"Look! She sitting next to her!" said Rayshaun from across the table.

The other kids at the table started buzzing just the way they had in our classroom that morning. I pretended not to hear them. I couldn't tell if Carli heard all that buzzing or not. If she did, she didn't act like it.

"Did you go to Hunter for kindergarten?" I asked. I didn't remember ever seeing her at school before.

I tore the clear plastic wrapper off my salad.

"No. I went to Highbridge Montessori School." She opened her juice box.

"Where's that at?"

"On the west side. In Eriewood."

"So how come you didn't go there for first grade?"

"Because of my papa's new job. He's a pharmacist."

"What's that?"

"He makes medicine for sick people. Papa said it didn't make sense to drive all the way across town every day. He said he could just find us an apartment in North Cleveland. Then he could get to his job easier."

"Oh."

"Papa says he doesn't care what people say about North Cleveland."

Carli took a great big bite of pizza.

I sipped some juice. Then I opened my little packet of Italian dressing and I poured dressing over my salad.

"He says Jane Hunter is a good school because it gets good scores," Carli said.

With her mouth full of pizza.

I wanted to tell her not to do that. Not to talk with her mouth full because she could choke. That's what Mama had always told me about talking with my mouth full. But I wasn't sure about saying anything to Carli because I thought maybe she wouldn't like me if I told her she could choke.

"I had kindergarten here," I said.

"Did you like it?"

Carli took another big bite of pizza. Even though she still had lots in her mouth from her last big bite. I got worried she might choke right there in the lunchroom.

"It was okay," I said, with Rayshaun Parker popping up in my brain. That boy had kind of ruined kindergarten for me. But I didn't tell Carli that.

"I hope I like it."

Carli's cheeks looked like she had two whole plums in there. I wished she ate smaller bites of food and chewed and swallowed them good like Mama had always told me to do.

I didn't feel right. I couldn't just watch that girl maybe choke herself even if she wouldn't like me for saying something.

"Carli?"

"Yes."

"Does your mother ever tell you you could choke if you eat like that?"

"No." Carli's cheeks still looked real fat. "My mother's dead."

I wasn't sure at all what to say about that information. I'd never met a girl with a dead mother before.

"Oh."

It was all I could think of.

I didn't know when they had stopped, but none of the kids at our table was buzzing anymore.

"I don't remember her," Carli said after a while.

"Hunh?"

"My mother. I don't remember what she looked like or anything. I mean, we have a picture of her on the wall at home. But I don't remember her inside my brain."

I got sad about what Carli was saying. I thought of my mama. I was glad I could remember her.

"How come you don't remember your mother?"

"I was too little when she died. I was a baby."

"Oh."

I stopped talking for a long time. I just ate my other slice of pizza and felt sad. But then I got another question for Carli:

"How come your mother is dead?"

"Papa said a man hit her car. He had drunk a lot of alcohol. So he crashed into my mother's car because of that. She died and my leg got busted up a lot. That's why I wear this."

146

Carli pointed to the thing on her leg. Parts of it were shiny, the same silvery color as forks and spoons. It had black parts on it, too. That thing was all over her whole leg. Up to under her dress. It looked Bionic, like the arm of the woman I'd seen on cable TV at my grandparents. But I'd seen Carli walk. That thing didn't make her leg move better than everybody else's like the Bionic Woman's arm did. It made her slower.

"What *is* that anyway?" I'd been wanting to ask that for a long time but I hadn't wanted to make her feel bad.

"A brace."

"What's it for?"

"It helps me walk."

"You can't walk without it?"

"I can a little. But I don't stand too straight. I fall."

"Oh."

After that, Carli and I just ate. We didn't talk. But my mind was skipping all over. I thought about kindergarten. Of how scared I felt after Rayshaun said I was going to hell. I thought of the scared look on Carli's face when she was in front of the classroom door that morning. I

147

thought of the mean laugh I heard in some kids'
voices when Carli showed up.

And I realized something: I was afraid of hearing that same laugh about me.

If Carli was ever going to drop me like
Rayshaun did or do that laugh at me, I wanted to
know right then.

"Carli?"

"Hm?"

"Are you Christian?"

"What?"

"Are you Christian?"

"I guess so. I mean, I don't know."

I waited. I waited to see if anything about
Carli's answer sounded scary—like it might turn
into a mean laugh or into saying I was going to
hell.

She started talking again.

"My grandpa and grandma are Christian.
They're my papa's parents. I know more Christian
people besides them, too. I mostly see them at
Christmas and Easter when Papa and I go to
church with Grandpa and Grandma. Some of
them are my cousins and aunts and uncles. Their
church is *so* pretty. It has these real tall glass win-

dows with lots of colors. They look like pictures made out of light."

I didn't say anything, in case she wasn't done.

Carli sipped her juice then sat it back down.

"Oh!" she said, like she had just remembered something. "And the Christian people? They make real good desserts. They even make their own *candy*. Daddy bought me some. It's good. How come you want to know?"

I wasn't all the way sure about Carli Flanagan, but I thought I should take a chance.

"Carli, I'm going to tell you something right now. So that you'll know. So that if you think it's funny or something, you and me don't have to be friends or anything."

"What?"

"I'm Buddhist."

"What's that?"

"My religion. I'm not Christian. I chant Nam Myoho Renge Kyo. My parents do, too."

Carli shrugged her shoulders.

"Okay."

"Okay?"

"Yeah. Okay."

CHAPTER 15

DRESSED LIKE A CANDIDATE

Forty minutes after I'd run off and left Carli on Bernard Avenue, I sat at the altar, alone at home, chanting like crazy. I hoped Carli wouldn't be so mad at me that she didn't come over. Mr. Flanagan wouldn't be home. She was supposed to stay at my house until he picked her up after work.

I chanted, but I could hardly think straight:

If it weren't for Carli, I wouldn't be in half the trouble I'm in now. That big old girl wouldn't be picking on me and I wouldn't have to look stupid trying to run for president. It's all Carli's fault!

... I hope she's okay.

Taneesha, if anything happens to Carli, it's your fault. You're supposed to walk home together. You *left* her!

That's over! In the past! What matters now is that she's safe. Carli, come over here, NOW! Even if you're mad at me! NAM MYOHO RENGE KYO!

The back door buzzed. I jumped up and ran into the kitchen. It was Carli! Her face was as red as hot salsa and if her eyes could talk, she could have been suspended for saying that at school.

But I didn't care. I was so happy to see her, I felt like doing Ronnie Lawson's twirling back-dance—only I didn't because she looked too dangerous.

We had a totally silent snack and study period.

Finally, sitting with my legs crossed lotus-style on the living room carpet, I couldn't take the quiet anymore.

"Well, if you still want to help me, I'm going to write a speech and make a flyer. I'll say why everybody should vote for me."

151

"And why *is* that anyway, Taneesha? You don't *want* to be president, remember?"

"Carli, I'm sorry." It felt good to let that out.

"What am I supposed to say to that girl, Taneesha? Hunh? I should tell her to leave you alone—so she can wallop *me*? 'Cause that's what she'll do, you know. She looks like she's a real good fighter. She might even be a boxer for all we know. Like Laila Ali or something. She's big enough."

What could I say? I knew she was right.

"We should *tell our parents*."

I couldn't put up a fight anymore. Carli made sense. Plus I could tell how badly she didn't want me to get every bone in my body ground to bits. Still, I believed I had good reasons not to totally cave in and tell my parents.

"Okay, okay," I said. "You can tell your father, but I'm not telling my parents. And I don't want you to either."

"Why?!"

"Carli, I know them. They'll say I should chant. That's what they say about everything. I hear their lectures and dumb little quotes all the time. It's always the same thing no matter what I'm going through. They don't listen.

"Plus if I tell them about that girl, they might come up to school. What good would that do? Once they leave, she can still beat me up. They can't be at school every day. They have to work!"

"I don't know…"

"You know what I'm saying, right, Carli? You see what it's like. I come home by myself—I mean with you, but you know what I mean. I make my snack by myself. I do my homework—all without my parents' help. Well mostly anyway."

"Your parents are nice, Taneesha. They do lots of stuff for you."

"That's not what I'm saying—" Couldn't she see? I didn't want my parents to get involved and then not be around to follow up. They didn't live in the school world, but I did. I couldn't depend on them to fix things when that world fell apart.

Those girls Carli and I saw fighting on Bernard yesterday had parents just like me. So did that boy we saw two weeks ago—the one who might be dead now, for all we knew.

But where were those parents? Not one grown-up helped those kids. People drove by in cars with their windows rolled up. They slowed down like they were watching reality TV.

It could be *me* next time. I could be the one alone on the street. I could be getting beat up after school with nobody to help me.

"Carli, I'm just saying I think I should at least try to handle this myself. On my own. Nobody can make one hundred percent sure that girl won't kick my butt. Not you. Not my parents, not anyone. I have to do it. If I can't, I'll tell them. But not yet."

"But you could get hurt."

"If I need help, I'll tell them, all right?"

My words hung in the air. Carli still seemed unconvinced.

After a while, I said, "What I need to do right now is make that dumb speech and a flyer. You going to help me or not?"

"You are so darn stubborn, Taneesha Bey-Ross."

By the time Carli and I shut down the computer we had a pretty decent speech and twenty-one flyer printouts (one for each kid and Mr. Alvarez):

154

VOTE 4 TANEESHA

She's friendly.
She's a good listener.
She's a hard worker.
She's all that and then some!
And she'll help you
with your schoolwork!

I practiced my speech with Carli playing audience and critic. We worked at it until Mr. Flanagan honked his car horn for Carli to come out.

"…One nation, under God, indivisible, with liberty and justice for all."

Wednesday, right after the Pledge of Allegiance, I took my seat and shot my hand into the air on one of the few occasions that I wore a skirt and tights to school—both navy blue. I had on a white blouse that I'd ironed myself—spray-starched and almost as crispy as Mr. Alvarez's shirt. That morning, I'd tried to dress like a candidate.

"Yes, Taneesha?" asked Mr. Alvarez, sounding

totally annoyed. "We have a lot to do today and we need to get started. What is it?"

I didn't need the embarrassment of asking my question in front of everyone.

Everybody's going to know that *you* know you blew it yesterday! Not that it's a *secret* or anything.

"Can I come to your desk? It's private."

"Oh, all right. Hurry now."

I popped out of my seat with my whole class staring at me. Mr. Alvarez didn't have to ask me twice to hurry. I didn't want to hear another "turtle" remark like yesterday.

"Can I give a new speech today?" I whispered when I got to his desk. "And pass out flyers?"

Everybody was so quiet it was spooky.

Trying to get all up in my conversation.

"Speeches were yesterday, Taneesha."

Can't you talk a little lower?

"As I said—" continued Mr. Alvarez.

Squirming, I wished I had stayed in my seat and kept my mouth shut.

"—we've got a very full schedule today."

Rayshaun and some other kids snickered. And suddenly, even though Mr. Alvarez was dogging me and I could hear them laughing behind me, I decided something: Mr. Alvarez *had* to let me give my speech again. I had to prove, to myself maybe, that I wasn't a flop, that I really *was* as big as the universe.

I straightened my back and held my head higher. I wasn't leaving that desk until that man gave me my "Yes."

"I know there's lots to do today but I didn't do my best yesterday. I wrote a better speech."

I didn't even bother trying to whisper.

If they hear me, they hear me.

Mr. Alvarez stared me right in the eyes.

I gave him just as good a look back.

Say "okay." Say "okay." Say "okay." Nam Myoho Renge Kyo!

I watched him begin to flip through his spiral planner notebook, taking *forever* to turn each page.

After a while, his eyes landed on mine again.

"Taneesha," he said slowly, "we don't have much time. But you can speak right after recess."

YES!

"Thank you! I don't need lots of time—just another chance! Thank you!"

I felt so light I nearly *flew* back to my desk seat. When I got there, I found a piece of paper folded on my chair. I sat and opened it.

I didn't tell my father.
—Carli

I smiled and looked over at Carli. She gave me a tiny wave.

After recess, Mr. Alvarez sat at his desk while I stood in front the class and read my speech:

"At first I didn't want to be class president. When Carli nominated me, I felt like saying, 'No way!' I thought being president would be too hard. I didn't think I was good enough to do the job. But I was wrong.

"Last week I had a great time on Take Your Child To Work Day. I went to the hospital where my mother works. I don't want to talk too much about it because I'm saving it for my report on Friday. But I will say I that had to work with children who have diabetes, a very serious illness.

"In our class, we've have been discussing leadership. We've learned that good leaders care about people, work hard, and try to make things better for everyone. We've learned that the best kind of

158

leader helps people become strong and bring out their own power so the people can be strong enough to help themselves and others, too.

"At the hospital, I read to children that are younger than me. Maybe when I read to them I made their day a little happier. They helped me, too. They helped me see that anyone can be brave—even little girls like them.

"Now I am going to be able to read to children at the hospital every week and I asked my mother if Carli can do it, too. I think that maybe Take Your Child To Work Day helped me develop the leadership skills I needed to help Carli become a volunteer at the hospital.

"If you elect me as your president, I will use my leadership skills to serve you. I will be friendly. I will be a good listener. I will help you with your schoolwork. I promise to work hard to help you bring out your power. I will also help you develop your leadership skills, too.

"Thank you!"

Mr. Alvarez smiled so bright I had to squint.

"Class, let's give Taneesha a well-deserved round of applause."

They did.

CHAPTER 16

SNAKE SNACK

Carli and I walked up Bernard Avenue after school. I'd been flying all afternoon, soaking up the glow of my classmate's praise ("Man, your speech was raw, Taneesha.") and the memory of all those claps that had seemed to go on and on for hours.

But the closer it got to the end of school, the less airborne I felt. By the time school let out, I'd crash-landed like a duck shot out of the sky.

Walking out of Hunter with Carli, all I could see was that older girl's fat, red jacket. And all I could feel was my chest caving in while her tank of a boot crushed it.

I started coughing.

"You all right?"

"Yeah. Well, no. But, yeah."

Earlier, at lunch, Carli had said she'd decided to wait and see how things went the rest of this week before telling her father what was going on. Now she and I headed up Bernard on the way home.

I looked at the clouds. It seemed like it might snow.

"Thanks again for not telling," I said, walking as fast as I could without pulling Carli behind me. She was holding on to my arm.

Even though I'd thanked her real naturally, inside, my feelings were as knotted as one of my locks. I was mad at her for having a limp and I felt selfish because of how I felt. I couldn't keep from thinking that if Carli's leg was normal we could have both run home before the older girl had a chance to sneak up on me.

"Well, like I said, I know you really don't want your parents to find out. As soon as I tell my father, he'll tell them for sure. I still think you're making a mistake, but—"

"Making *what* mistake? I told you you is

161

dumb, girl. Even your little cripple friend know it." The older girl forced her way between Carli and me, splitting us apart. "What you mess up?"

"Excuse me?" I asked, irked.

"You heard me. I said, 'What you mess up?'"

"I didn't mess up anything."

I felt confused. I didn't have a clue what she was raging about this time. I wondered what excuse she would use now to smear misery all over an otherwise okay day.

"You lying. What I tell you about lying to me? Cripple Girl said you made a mistake and I know she right, 'cause all you is is one ugly mistake. I bet your mama think so, too."

Suddenly, the girl's voice sounded familiar. Not because I'd been listening to her on the street for the past few weeks but because I'd heard her a lot of times before. From inside. *She sounded just like Evella.* Her words were sort of different, and so was her voice, but no doubt about it, she was feeding me the same junk Evella did. Only instead of being in my head, the girl—or was it Evella?—was live and in person, right on Bernard Avenue.

And I was not having it this time.

"No! My mama doesn't think I'm a mistake!

For your information, my mama says I'm big as the universe.

"And *she* is not a cripple!" I said, pointing to Carli.

The sound of my own voice was just the *oomph* I needed to do some raging myself. "You know what? You're nothing but a mean bully, picking on kids smaller than you! You're—you're just a coward!"

"Oh no you *didn't* just call me a coward! If I'm a coward, then I'm the coward that's going to beat your ugly little butt!"

Before I knew it, the older girl shoved me and I stumbled backwards, into the street. I hit the asphalt *hard*. Hard enough to rattle my bones. I lay still, too stunned to move. Cars rolled by and honked at me.

What she'd do *that* for?

I wasn't sure if something was broken on me or not.

Carli gasped and helped me up. We got back onto the sidewalk.

I guess nothing's broken.

All my bones moved okay. I shook my head back and forth, trying to get my senses together.

Next thing I knew, the older girl reached for me again.

No. Stop! Help! Heeeeeeeeeelp!

I looked left and right, trying to see how to get past the incredible hulk that was moving in on me fast—

"Surprise! Hey, hop in girls!"

Phew! Mama's dark blue minivan pulled up along the curb!

"I got off work a little early today!" she hollered from her rolled-down window. "I came by to pick you two up!"

THANK YOU, MAMA!

I would have shouted my gratitude but I didn't want to seem like a baby in front of the older girl, or in front of Carli, for that matter.

"Don't think it's over! I'll be back for you." The older girl spat her words at me through clenched teeth.

I skittered by her like a roach caught in light, running from a can of Raid. Carli followed behind me.

When I passed the older girl, she growled in my ear so that only I heard her. "No little kid's going to talk to *me* like that!"

Carli and I leaped in the minivan's beige, middle-row seats.

"Hey, you girls all right? You're huffing and puffing like the Big Bad Wolf." Mama chuckled a little. Wearing her black coat and earmuffs, she eased the minivan into the driving lane. "Why are you so out of breath?"

I bucked my eyes at Carli and held my index finger to my lips.

Carli mouthed, "*Why not?!*" flumped her back onto her seat, and pressed her lips together as if that pushed her words inside.

"We—we were just—we were—rushing to get in the van!" Realizing that I probably sounded like I was freaking out, which I was, I took a breath and slowed down. "I guess that tired us out."

"Really? You girls are young. Don't scare me saying you poop-out that fast. You should be in better shape than that."

Please, no Officer HP today.

"We're all right, Mama. We were walking pretty fast before you pulled up."

Everything that had just happened swirled in my head. I caught Mama's eye in the rearview mirror.

"You sure you're all right, honey? You look kind of sick. We better take your temperature when we get home."

"I'm okay. Just thinking about all the homework I have to do, that's all." I sighed. I wanted to tell my mother what was going on. But instead, I said, "Oh. I gave my campaign speech today. For class president."

"Yeah? How'd it go?"

"She did a great job," sighed Carli.

"Carli helped a lot," I mumbled.

"Well, neither one of you sound like it. You sound like the living dead."

I couldn't even manage a fake laugh at Mama's joke. Fear swallowed me in one big gulp.

"Who was that girl you were talking to?"

"Hunh?"

"That girl you were talking to when I pulled up. Who was she?"

"Oh, her?" I gave Carli a "Now what?!" look.

She shrugged her shoulders and pressed her lips tighter.

"Who was she, honey?"

"Um, she... she...I...I...I dropped a pencil sharpener out of my pocket!" I blurted. "She picked it up. She was just giving it back to me."

The van had stopped at a red light. In the mirror, Mama looked into my eyes—obviously buying none my story.

The minivan's walls squeezed in from all sides, suffocating me. I waited for my mother's next question. It never came.

I exhaled.

"Well, I finagled a few hours off today," Mama said, after a few minutes. "One of the nurses switched with me. I have to come in early tomorrow to make up for it, though."

I barely heard her. The older girl's threat throbbed in my head: "I'll be back for you!" I felt like the scared little mouse I once saw cornered by a boa constrictor at the zoo.

You wouldn't be in this mess if you had kept your big mouth shut!

Snake snack. That's me.

"Taneesha, you've got to tell your parents!" whispered Carli, sitting on the living room floor with me at my house while we pretended to study. I'd changed into jeans, a grey sweatshirt, and my lavender bunny slippers. Carli still had on her school clothes—white sweater, navy pants.

"Okay. Okay. You're right. I'll tell them tonight."

"Why don't we just do it now? While I'm here? This is serious. That girl pushed you into the street! You could have gotten run over! She was going to hit you!"

"I don't want to tell them yet, Carli. But I will tonight. Promise. Can you do me one last favor?"

"What?"

"I'll call you after I talk to my parents. Can you wait until then to tell your father?"

"Taneesha!"

"Please, Carli. I'm going to tell them tonight, I swear. I just don't want them to find out from your father first."

"You'll call me?"

"Promise."

"All right."

Now things were even more complicated. My parents would want to know why I hadn't told them about the girl before. I didn't know what I'd say to them but I knew Carli was right. I had to say something.

The rest of the day came and went like always. Mr. Flanagan picked up Carli. My parents and I ate dinner. Everything was the same as usual except for the fact that all I could think about was how tomorrow that girl might stomp the life out of me with her army tank boots.

CHAPTER 17

INVISIBLE, COZY BLANKET

"TANEESHA IMANI BEY-ROSS! PLEASE COME DOWNSTAIRS!"

I flinched. I'd been in my bedroom laying out clothes for tomorrow and I knew that Mama screeching my whole name could only mean trouble.

I'd planned to tell my parents everything as soon as I finished getting my clothes together. Really. I had. But now I had a sick feeling that I'd put the conversation off a little too long.

Moments later, I stood in the living room facing them. They sat on the edge of the green couch—Mama in a red pullover and jeans, Daddy in a white shirt and navy pants, grinding his teeth.

"Have a seat," he said, patting the space between him and Mama while the veins on the side of his temples bulged.

I did not like the vibe in that room at all. If I sat on that couch, I'd be trapped between them.

"That's okay. I'll stand."

"Taneesha, honey—" Mama began. Even though her face seemed a little softer than Daddy's, her eyes scanned me like a lie detector. "—is there something you want to tell us?"

I glanced around, up and down, as if I'd find the answer to that question on the ceiling or something.

"Something I want to tell you? Like what?"

"Anything unusual happen after school?" Daddy asked through his teeth.

"Unusual?"

I could have sworn I heard one of Daddy's molars crack.

"Taneesha, Carli's father just called," he said, matter-of-factly. "According to him, an older girl's been threatening you after school. Why didn't you tell us?" With this question, his edginess dissolved and the only thing left on his face was concern—and maybe disappointment.

Now the couch seemed safe. I flopped down between them with a huff.

"Carli was supposed to wait."

"What?" asked Daddy, sounding confused.

"I told her I was going to tell you myself. She was supposed to wait before she said anything to her father."

I was glad to be able to pin some blame off me.

"Well, that's beside the point, Taneesha," said Daddy, annoyed. "It's a good thing Carli told. Now please explain what's going on."

"Please honey. Why didn't you tell us?" Mama sounded so pitiful you'd have thought everything was her fault. "We want to help," she said.

Guilt tugged at me.

I didn't want to say anything to hurt my parent's feelings.

But, then again, I didn't want to hear another lecture either—and that was always a possibility with them, no matter how touchy-feely they were acting at that moment. Plus, hadn't they both just asked why I didn't tell them what was going on? How could they even think a crazy question like that?

"Why didn't I tell you? I couldn't because—"

"What do you mean, you couldn't, Taneesha?" Mama butted in.

There she goes—again.

"I mean, it's not like I can just talk to you and Daddy—"

"What's that supposed to mean?"

There he goes again.

"You talk to us all the time," Mama said.

"No, Mama, you talk—"

"Of, course. I'm your mother. Mothers and daughters should talk."

"And Daddy talks."

"I'm your father. Fathers and daughters should talk, too."

"But—"

"But what?!" they both butted in, dagnamit!

"YOU DON'T LISTEN! I CAN'T EVEN TALK TO YOU RIGHT NOW. AND WHENEVER YOU DO LET ME GET A WORD IN, NO MATTER WHAT'S HAPPENING, YOU TELL ME THE SAME THING—CHANT! I KNEW THAT'S WHAT YOU'D SAY! SO WHY BOTHER TELLING YOU?

"AND ANYWAY, I *HAVE* BEEN CHANTING. ON MY *OWN*. EVEN WITHOUT YOU *FORCING* ME TO! HAH! THAT'S IT, RIGHT? THAT'S *ALL* I GOT TO DO! AND I'M *DOING* IT! SO I DON'T NEED YOUR HELP!"

I shlumped my back against the couch, panting.

My parents didn't say anything.

I couldn't tell if they were mad or what.

We sat there like that for a long time. I didn't look at them. My shoulders sagged. I kept my eyes on my hands—they drooped over my thighs like empty gloves.

"Well, Taneesha," Mama said, finally, "it seems like you have things under control."

Hey. She didn't sound mad.

"But—" Daddy began.

He was only getting one word in; still, I noticed he didn't use his angry voice to say it.

Strange.

"*And,*" Mama barreled over Daddy, "your father and I appreciate your honesty."

I noticed how Mama said each word extra slowly—as if she thought I'd break apart if she spoke normally. I started thinking that maybe she thought I was cracking up or something.

Maybe they weren't just being nice. Maybe they were afraid. Afraid they had a daughter with a few chocolate chips missing from her cookie.

"Our concern is, however," Mama said, "that this girl sounds like she might hurt you, Taneesha. At least that's the way Carli described her."

Now I got it. They *were* scared. They were afraid I'd be hurt.

Boy, was I lucky. I could have been on lock-down for life the way I'd just talked to them.

I watched them, though. I had to make sure they stayed level-headed. I knew those two; they could switch up on me fast.

"We can't just let you get hurt, Taneesha," Mama said.

"I don't want to get hurt either."

That was true. I saw an opening. A chance to explain myself more without screaming—and risking my parents ditching the understanding-parent bit.

"But—" I said.

"Good," said Mama. "I'm glad we have a point we all agree on. That being the case, why

175

don't I come up to the school tomorrow? Just to check out everything and—"

My palms and underarms got sweaty. I had to make them see the spot I was in.

"Mama, you know what? I want you to come. That girl said she'd beat me up and I believe her. But I'm afraid if she gets mad at me because I told on her, she'll do something even worse. You'll be at work then. Kids get jumped after school all the time. Their parents aren't there or anything."

I paused, hoping I could somehow make a thing happen that probably wouldn't. I ducked my head, squeenched my eyebrows, and I peeked up at my mother. Batting my eyes like a puppy, I made the saddest face I could without practicing in a mirror.

"Mama, can you pick me up every day?"

She looked uncomfortable. Guilty, maybe.

"No, honey," she said, softy. "I can't do that. I don't have that kind of schedule."

"I didn't think so."

See.

I knew they couldn't help. Not really.

You're on your own, Taneesha.

"Well, if the situation's that bad," Daddy's voice crashed in like a wrecking ball, "then that girl needs serious help. Maybe she should be suspended or expelled or get counseling or something. I don't care what's going on. We can't just have her bullying you and do nothing about it."

Hearing Macho Man, I perked up. Maybe I *would* live to see sixth grade. Lately, I was beginning to wonder about that.

"Your father's right, Taneesha. We'll get the principal involved, her parents, whatever's necessary. But we've got to do something, honey. We have to protect you. That's our job."

In that moment, an invisible, cozy blanket wrapped around me and I realized something: It was true, I had to face life on my own. But I wasn't *alone*. Even when my parents weren't with me, their love was. And it always would be.

"Tell you what," said Mama, "how about we chant? Oops!" She slapped her hands over her mouth. "That one slipped out, didn't it?"

We all laughed.

"That's okay, Mama. I was thinking the same thing. But first I want to read something."

I sat in the center chair in front of the altar with my parents sitting on either side of me. In the Gosho lying opened on the altar table, I'd found the page I wanted. I read:

> Bodhisattva Never Disparaging was for many years cursed and humiliated, beaten with sticks and staves, and pelted with tiles and stones by countless people because he honored them by uttering…: "I have profound reverence for you, I would never dare treat you with disparagement or arrogance. Why? Because you are all practicing the bodhisattva way and are certain to attain Buddhahood"… Those who belittled and cursed Never Disparaging acted that way at first, but later they deeply respected him.

I closed the Gosho, and, even without looking at my parents, I knew they were smiling. So was I. I'd read that passage because I wanted to. And I read it to say "Thank you" to them.

I bonged the bell and we all started chanting. A warm, tingly feeling glowed from inside of me and spread all over. My body and mind danced together to the rhythm of my voice.

Okay, girl with no name. So you're a Buddha, huh? At least that's what Never Disparaging says. He says we're all Buddhas. Even when we're mean, or stupid, or say dumb stuff. Even when we're bullies.

Tell you what: Tomorrow will be a good day. I promise. I'll make it a good day for all of us.

CHAPTER 18

STANDING O

On Thursday, next thing I knew, school was over way too fast for me. It seemed like 2:55 rolled around before my bottom hit the seat good in 509.

I hadn't won the day's election. Ronnie Lawson did—even though everybody had given me all that applause yesterday. But I had too much on my mind to care a whole lot about how losing totally stank.

Now kids, in all kinds of jackets and coats, were spilling out of Hunter like multicolored laundry powder from a box turned upside down. Carli and I walked toward the school building's beige brick wall and waited there for our parents.

Shivering, I jammed my hands into my coat pockets and hunched my shoulders, shifting my weight from left to right. I kept doing that, trying to keep warm. I looked up at the dull, gray sky.

Man, I miss the sun.

Then, a few yards in front of me, I saw something that hit me like a punch in the stomach.

"Look, Carli," I pointed in front of us, at Bernard Avenue.

A giant tree had fallen clear across the street. It backed up traffic in both directions. Five firefighters hacked at the humungous trunk. There was no way Mama and Mr. Flanagan could get through. I felt doomed.

"I hope our parents can get to us in time." I said.

I bet I sounded doomed.

"Yeah, me too."

Carli definitely sounded doomed.

I started thinking up a Plan B.

Maybe Carli and I should go into the building to wait. But Mrs. Andrews…The secretary will get mad at us…

Scaredy-cat, scaredy-cat, you going to get your butt kicked!

181

I AM NOT GOING TO GET MY BUTT KICKED!

I almost jumped at the sound of me. I shook my head a little, surprised. Then I said it again: I AM NOT GOING TO GET MY BUTT KICKED!

Suddenly, I felt free and bodacious, like a galloping horse.

"Uh-oh," Carli moaned. "Guess who's coming down the street."

In slow motion, I turned toward the direction Carli nodded at. I didn't have to guess. I knew who I'd see.

Okay? Now what? *RUN!*

I saw that big old girl walking, staring at me, looking like a dog with rabies—crazy, and almost foaming at the mouth.

My bodaciousness flew away.

"Nam Myoho Renge Kyo! Nam Myoho Renge Kyo! Nam Myoho Renge Kyo!" Without thinking, I'd started chanting quietly, fast and fierce.

"What did you say?"

"I said, I'm *not* running! I'm going to stand right here and face that girl!"

"Okay. Then I'll stand with you."

I looked at Carli quickly, then we both went back to watching doom approach.

182

She walked along the sidewalk across the street. Her pit-bull eyes sliced into me. She kept coming.

The firefighters had finally chopped the tree into big chunks. They cleared its pieces from the street. Half of it lay on Carli's and my side of Bernard, half on the other. Firefighters directed traffic.

The older girl started crossing over, zig-zagging through cars that crawled along Bernard's muddy layer of snow slush.

I stood still, ready to grab Carli's hand and take off up the street if I needed to.

With her eyes glued to me, the older girl stepped up and over the curb. Before I could duck, her fist flew.

Suddenly, her feet slid around on a patch of ice. She lost her balance and fell facedown onto a shoveled part of the concrete sidewalk.

Right at my feet.

I heard the hard thud that must have rattled her bones and I jerked back.

I remembered the fall I'd had just like hers yesterday. The fall I had because she *pushed* me.

Yeah! Now you know how it *feels!*

I soaked up the sight of her, my enemy, lying

on the sidewalk. I drank in every sweet drop of *revenge*. It tasted even better than guava-mango juice. *Delicious*.

The girl got to her knees slowly, as if it hurt to move.

I looked down at her as she sucked blood from her lip.

And something moved inside of me.

As big as she was, she seemed kind of helpless.

I blinked and opened my eyes wide to focus. Did I see a tear fall?

What was I *thinking*? I'd just acted like somebody I didn't know. I'd *laughed* over her pain. It was as if I'd turned into Evella—only worse. As if, for a few moments, I was somebody I didn't like. Somebody I *never* wanted to be.

I stooped down to help the girl up. Carli did, too.

"Get away from me! I don't need y'all's help!" The girl struggled on the ground for a moment, like she was fighting the concrete.

Finally, she made it to her feet and started brushing dirt and snow off her coat. She straightened out her black backpack.

Then she glanced toward the sidewalk.

I saw her notice something there. She gave Carli and me a quick look. I could tell she didn't want us to see what she saw.

But I did see.

The girl swooped down to the ground and crouched over a small blue pouch. The two medical needles and glucose meter lying near the pouch on the sidewalk must have fallen out of it.

That's her stuff?

Peeking sideways at me, she waddled like a duck, snatching up everything, and quickly stuffed the needles and meter into the pouch. She pulled its drawstring closed, stood, wriggled one backpack strap off her arm, and tugged her backpack sideways in front of her. Then she tucked the pouch into one of the backpack's side pockets, zipped the pocket, and returned the backpack to its place behind her.

Her eyes narrowed into hardened slits. "What y'all looking at?!"

I pictured Ebony, Shantay, and Loren at the hospital. They'd used the same kind of needles as the older girl's.

I looked her straight in the eye. I wasn't sure if I should say anything but I decided to try.

"Do you—do you have diabetes?"

"Taneesha, let's just walk away." Carli sounded as if she thought I was lucky to still be alive.

"None of your business what I got."

I shrank. Why had I even bothered? I was ready to take Carli's advice and cut out.

"And anyway," the girl said, with a sort of softer mean face, "what you know about diabetes?"

Hey, I'm not a little kid. Okay. Here goes again: "My mother's a nurse."

I hoped my big announcement impressed her. I hoped she could tell that it wasn't like I was some dumb little kid that didn't know anything.

But a second later, the big "SO WHAT?" all over her face killed my hopes.

How could I convince her that I knew what I was talking about?

"I met kids with diabetes at the hospital where my mother works," I blurted. "I know sometimes people with diabetes take shots to keep from getting sick. They need um, um…" *Dang!* My mind scrambled to think of the name of— "*Insulin!* They need *insulin.* Is that why you've got needles?"

"What's it like having diabetes?" Carli asked.

186

I watched that girl fighting to stay tough—and losing the fight.

Then she sighed like she'd been holding her breath all her life.

"I'm just finding out myself. I got it all of a sudden. The doctor say my body don't use sugar like it's supposed to. All I know is I can't eat like normal people." She looked downward. I could hardly hear her when she said, "Y'all probably want to laugh at me, right?"

I shook my head slowly. Carli did the same thing.

A wave of relief washed over the girl's face. "I don't know about those people at your mother's job—" She spoke as if truth was rising up out of well deep inside of her. "—but I hate having to take a bunch of stupid shots all the time. I was scared if anybody found out I'm sick they'd think I'm weird. So I ain't told none of my friends."

I wanted to tell her that I understood but the words stayed locked inside me.

"Well, if they're really your friends," said Carli, "they won't mind if you're different. Real friends stick by each other."

Carli's words nudged me to speak.

187

"She's right. Friends don't care about stuff like that. Everybody's got some type of problem. Anybody mean enough to make fun of you for having diabetes's not your friend anyway."

The girl seemed to think about that.

But that wasn't all.

I could tell something else pulled at chains inside her.

"Sometimes…" she whispered.

Then she stopped, like maybe she wasn't sure she should go on.

But then she did.

"Sometimes I'd rather die than have this dumb disease."

There was silence after that.

The three of us stood still.

A light snow began to fall.

Snowflakes softly landed like cool feathers on my cheeks and melted.

The girl raised her eyes until they met mine, and Carli's, too.

The girl exhaled and a tiny cloud appeared and vanished in front of her face.

"Sorry," she said, with her head hung low. "Sorry I been so mean to y'all. I guess—I guess I been in kind of a bad mood."

And then I *knew*. I knew what I had to do. Not only to help her break free, but for me, too.

"That's okay. I get in bad moods, too, sometimes."

"Yeah. Me too," said Carli.

The girl looked at us. And that was it. I could see just who she was.

"Uh...my name's...my name's Jewel."

I smiled so wide that the crisp air hurt my stretching face. But I didn't mind at all.

"I'm Taneesha."

"And I'm Carli." She was all teeth, too.

Just then, Mama's minivan zoomed to a stop along the curb. Mr. Flanagan's green car pulled up fast behind her.

Windows slid down.

"Taneesha, you all right?!"

I heard a solid promise in Mama's worried voice: "If you got a problem, I got your back."

"Is everything okay, Carli?" dittoed Mr. Flanagan.

"We're fine!" I stood there cheesing like a girl in a Colgate commercial.

All of a sudden, out pops Mr. Sun, sailing

from behind a cloud and scattering shimmery beads of light on the falling snowflakes. I felt warm from the inside out and the whole world shined especially for me.

I smiled at Carli and Jewel. Then I turned and waved at Mama and Mr. Flanagan and said, "Thanks! We'll see you at home!"

I was ready to burst I was so excited. It was a Friday and I had a guest to bring to Ontario Hospital! Exactly four weeks ago, I'd given my famous Take Your Child To Work Day report at school. And guess what? I got a standing O! In fact, because of my report, 509 put together group projects on diabetes prevention—keeping kids from getting diabetes. We presented it to the whole school, too! My mother was our guest speaker. Thank you very much, Officer HP.

That Friday, four weeks ago, also happened to be the first day Carli and I volunteered as official story readers for kids at Ontario Hospital. Since then, every Friday, we'd been walking to the hospital after school.

Today, I led the guest through Ontario's hallways. I never knew how many children would be waiting for me from one week to the next.

The guest and I walked into the large children's room. With all beds filled, six little faces stared up at us—four boys and two girls. Carli was already there, sitting in a chair in front of the children.

"Hi, boys and girls," I said, waving.

The kids waved and Hi-ed back.

"Shantay, you know me already. But everybody else, I'm Taneesha. I read books here with Carli."

I opened my hand palm up toward the visitor the way game-show models do on TV when they're showing off the grand prize. "And this is a good friend of ours. She's going to read with us today. And guess what? She has diabetes just like you. Everybody, say hi to Jewel."

I pressed my hands together and bowed to Jewel—Japanese-style, the way Natsuko bows. The way Daisaku Ikeda bows. And for just a second—a second like eternity, like forever—I thought I heard Bodhisattva Never Disparaging.

I heard that guy clapping, giving me a standing O.

191

THE END

ACKNOWLEDGMENTS

I deeply thank the following people for helping *Taneesha Never Disparaging* become a reality: Josh Bartok, Laura Cunningham, Joe Evans, Tony Lulek, and everyone at Wisdom Publications, for believing in Taneesha and warmly welcoming her onto their list; writers Rhenee McGraw-Harris and Christine Taylor-Butler, for providing honest and essential feedback; the staff, faculty, and participants of the Highlights Foundation 2006 writers' workshop in Chautauqua, New York, with special thanks to Rich Wallace and Jerry Spinelli, for their affirmations and perfect tweaking advice; editor Eileen Robinson of F1rstPages.com, whose caring, thorough, and frank expertise enabled me to dig deeper and go further; Regina Brooks of

195

SerendipityLit.com, the best agent I never had, for a critique that was like good medicine—hard to take but effective; Kathleen Bernetich, for lovingly igniting my writing career; Mayumi Rindflesch, for sharing Haru Jenkins's story; Haru Jenkins, for living, remembering, and telling the history that became Natsuko's memories (although Haru dresses up more than Natsuko, and her hair isn't orange, she *does* look like a girl when she smiles); Linda Johnson, for the "never be defeated" encouragement that gave rise to Evella; the staff of the Cleveland Clinic's Huron Hospital Lennon Diabetes Center in East Cleveland, for patiently answering my medical questions; my family members and friends, for endless love and support; and Daisaku Ikeda, for being my Sensei.

Excerpts from *The Writings of Nichiren Daishonin, Volume I* appear courtesy of the publisher, Soka Gakkai (The Gosho Translation Committee, Translator, Tokyo, 2000). The quotations are from the following writings: "Reply to Kyo'o"; "On Attaining Buddhahood in this Lifetime"; "Letter to the Sage Nichimyo"; and "Letter from Sado." The actual sentence from "Letter from

Sado" reads: "Those who belittled and cursed Never Disparaging acted that way at first, but later they took faith in his teachings and willingly became his followers."

The real title of the book of poetry that is mentioned in this story is *Fighting for Peace—Poems by Daisaku Ikeda* (Andrew Gebert, Translator, Dunhill Publishing, CA, 2004).

Excerpts from the poem "Peace and Happiness for All!—A Prayer for Lasting World Peace" by Daisaku Ikeda appear in *Taneesha Never Disparaging* courtesy of the Soka Gakkai. The poem originally appeared in the April 8, 2003, issue of the *Seikyo Shimbun*, the Soka Gakkai daily newspaper in Japan.

ABOUT THE AUTHOR

M. LAVORA PERRY'S words have been tucked inside envelops and mailed around the world because she used to write greeting cards. She's the coauthor of *Teen Sister's Health—A Body, Mind, & Spirit Wellness Guide for Girls of Color* and she's working on her second novel for young people, *Hidden Jewel*. Ms. Perry likes reading, writing, watermelon, and riding her purple bike as much as Taneesha likes her magenta one. She lives with her husband and three children in Ohio. Visit her website at mlavoraperry.com.

About Wisdom Publications

Wisdom Publications, a nonprofit publisher, is dedicated to making available authentic works relating to Buddhism for the benefit of all.

To learn more about Wisdom, or to browse books online, visit our website at www.wisdompubs.org.

You may request a copy of our catalog online or by writing to this address:

Wisdom Publications
199 Elm Street
Somerville, Massachusetts 02144 USA
Telephone: 617-776-7416
Fax: 617-776-7841
Email: info@wisdompubs.org
www.wisdompubs.org

THE WISDOM TRUST

As a nonprofit publisher, Wisdom is dedicated to the publication of Dharma books for the benefit of all sentient beings and dependent upon the kindness and generosity of sponsors in order to do so. If you would like to make a donation to Wisdom, you may do so through our website or our Somerville office. If you would like to help sponsor the publication of a book, please write or email us at the address above.

Thank you.

Wisdom is a nonprofit, charitable 501(c)(3) organization affiliated with the Foundation for the Preservation of the Mahayana Tradition (FPMT).